'Uni... ...ly
and full of drama.
Genius!'
Closer

Helen loves boyfriend Phil so why, with only a week to
go, has she yet to buy her wedding dress? Convinced it's
a case of cold feet, she lets best friend Yaz talk her into
celebrating with a hen weekend at a luxury spa hotel.

Arriving at The Manor, Helen is expecting a weekend
of champagne, pampering and laughs with old friends.
The one thing she hasn't planned for is running into
her ex fiancé, the man who broke her heart,
the man who has a secret he's desperate to share.

And then of course there's what the boys
are up to in Amsterdam...

Told as two separate stories that have implications
for both Helen and Phil's future happiness,
The Stag and Hen Weekend is a fresh and
original story of a couple trying to get it right and
all too often getting it spectacularly wrong.

Mike Gayle is the author of ten bestselling novels and
has contributed to a variety of magazines including *FHM*,
Sunday Times Style and *Cosmopolitan*.

NOW
TURN
OVER

Also available
as an ebook

THE HEN WEEKEND

MIKE GAYLE

HODDER

First published in Great Britain in 2012 by Hodder & Stoughton
An Hachette UK company

First published in paperback in 2013

1

Copyright © 2012 Mike Gayle

A CIP catalogue record for this title is available
from the British Library

ISBN 978 1 444 70860 8 (B format)
ISBN 978 1 444 76855 8 (A format)

Printed and bound by Clays Ltd, St Ives plc

Hodder & Stoughton policy is to use papers that are natural,
renewable and recyclable products and made from wood grown
in sustainable forests. The logging and manufacturing processes
are expected to conform to the environmental regulations
of the country of origin.

Hodder & Stoughton Ltd
338 Euston Road
London NW1 3BH

www.hodder.co.uk

For C.

Acknowledgements

Thanks to Sue Fletcher, Swati Gamble, and all at Hodder, Phil Gayle, the Sunday Night Pub Club, Jackie Behan, the Board and above all, to C, for pretty much everything.

Friday

1.

It had been three hours since Phil had left for Amsterdam, an hour since she had dropped Samson off at the kennels and Helen Richards was now staring, in a bewildered fashion, down at her open weekend suitcase. In one hand she held a Braun hairdryer and in the other a brand new pair of GHD hair-straighteners. Her ability to get maximum enjoyment from the coming weekend was contingent on both items making the journey to Ashbourne with her, but as the case was already full of belongings deemed so essential that she had opted to pack them *before* her hairdryer and straighteners it was clear that the only options open to her were upgrading to a larger case (something which Yaz, who had agreed to drive half of the party to their weekend destination, had specifically forbidden) or to spend the last weekend of her unmarried existence in a state of abject frizzy-haired misery.

Paralysed by indecision, she was saved by the ringing of her mobile. She dropped the items in her hands on top of the case, picked up her phone from the bed and glanced at the screen, convinced it would be Phil calling to update her on his journey. It wasn't Phil, however, it was Yaz.

Helen and the forthright Turkish-born, Cleethorpes-raised Yaz had been friends for many years. Starting out their careers in radio as broadcast assistants at the same local station in Nottingham, they had bonded over a shared sense of humour and love of red wine. Over the weeks that followed, their friendship continued to grow, and driven by a desperate need to find an affordable place to live so that they could stop sleeping on friends' sofas, they had scoured the lower end of the accommodation food chain until they came across 111 Jevonbrook Road, a large, dilapidated terraced house without any form of central heating situated in the Lenton area of the city. Despite the cold, the mould and the guy no one seemed to know who took up residence in their kitchen, Helen loved those days, reminiscing fondly about how they would party until dawn, crawl into bed for a few hours, work a full day and then start the partying all over again. With Yaz even the dullest day ended up with them having a giggle or some weird encounter which would entertain them for months.

All these years later, having moved homes and changed jobs several times, they were both back in the city in which they had met. Yaz was now a full-time mum to two small children living the suburban dream in a modern four-bedroom semi as close as humanly possible to the best primary school in the area and Helen, following a bad break-up, had devoted herself to her career and was now the presenter of her own pre-drivetime afternoon show, *The Chat* with Helen Richards, on BBC Radio Sherwood.

'All packed?' enquired Yaz.

Helen looked down at the suitcase in front of her. 'Nearly. A few last minute issues but nothing I can't handle. How about you?'

'Did it last night while the kids were asleep. I knew I'd never have the time today because mornings are always so mental around here. Plus I'm entertaining Simon's mum as she's babysitting for the weekend. I'm sure I'll get to the hotel and find out that I've forgotten half the things I need but I can always buy what's missing. After all, that's why they invented shopping.'

'You'll be fine,' said Helen. 'How many times have we been away together and I've never once seen you forget a single thing? Who was it who pulled out a tube of superglue when Katie's heel broke off while we were out for her birthday? You're the living embodiment of "Be Prepared!" '

'Was Simon on time to pick up Phil? I bet he wasn't. I told him last night to fill up the car and go to the cash point and he was like "Yeah, yeah, yeah," and then what's the last thing he said to me this morning after sloping out of bed at half nine when I'd been up since six getting the kids ready for school, making their sandwiches, doing the school run *and* tidying up the spare bedroom for his Mum's arrival? "Oh, I think I'm going to need to fill up the car and get some money out." ' Yaz sighed. 'They'd be lost without us wouldn't they?'

'Hopelessly so.'

'Anyway, I was just calling to let you know that I got a text from Dee to say that she's got this work thing she's got to do and could we leave half an hour later than arranged. I was going to do a whole group text thing to let the rest of the girls know but I honestly couldn't be bothered with all that typing.'

Even though they would be seeing each other in an hour Helen and Yaz continued chatting because that was the relationship they had. They were friends who spoke about anything and everything, often two or three times a day, with no excuse needed and although on the surface Yaz appeared to be the more dominant of the two, scratch below the façade and it became apparent that theirs was a relationship of equals.

They talked about the weekend and how much they were looking forward to it and Yaz confessed that she had even dreamt about it and was about to give Helen the full details when the conversation was cut short by the howling of a small boy, who had just banged his head on the table while playing armies with his older brother.

Helen tossed the phone on the bed and returned to her suitcase dilemma before recalling that she was now in possession of an extra half-hour which might be put to best use by the drinking of a cup of tea and the eating of a consolatory milk chocolate Hobnob.

As the kettle boiled and she hunted in the cupboard

for her favourite mug she pondered the dirty jokes, filthy laughter, luminous cocktails and dancing on tables of past hen dos. How long since she had been on one? Years, surely. And there had been some good ones too. Yaz's infamous weekend in Blackpool, Helen's cousin Esme's one in London that had ended with two girls being arrested for indecent exposure and not forgetting her first ever hen do when an old school friend had invited her to her last hurrah at the local Yates's Wine Lodge in Doncaster when they were both nineteen. Good times each and every one. But perhaps unsurprisingly the one that she dwelt on longest was the worst one of her life: her own, some ten years earlier, for the wedding that never was.

Helen and her former fiancé Aiden Reid had met at work. Although she had been attracted to him from the very first moment she had spotted him in the canteen at BBC Radio Merseyside, Helen never considered, even for a fleeting second, that any relationship that might result from their dating might end in a marriage proposal, because while Aiden was undoubtedly driven, charming and utterly beguiling, one thing of which she and even the most deluded of women would agree upon was that he was not exactly marriage material. A fact to which he attested.

'Last night was a laugh wasn't it?' he told her on the doorstep as he prepared to leave after their first night together. 'But you know I'm not looking for anything serious, don't you?'

Helen laughed. 'Believe me Mr Deluded if I was in

the market for something serious yours would be the last door that I would come knocking on.'

'Because you don't think I can do serious?'

'No,' said Helen, 'because I know so.'

And so even as they graduated from casual fun-filled fling to a state of existence where Aiden spent more nights at her home than he did in his own, Helen remained resolutely indifferent to any talk of the future. What they had was fun and light-hearted, which proved a great relief from their stressful day-to-day jobs as overworked production assistants regularly putting in thirteen-hour days, often six days a week in order to prove themselves and climb a little further up the career ladder.

But, as is often the case in these situations, somewhere between Aiden's increasingly playful daydreams ('It's such a shame you're on the pill because you and me would make some right proper beautiful babies,') and Helen's emotional detachment ('I don't care if you're here all the time I don't want you leaving your stuff here,') a compromise was struck, and the daydreams became less abstract, the emotions more engaged until finally they both realised that they had managed to somehow fall in love.

The proposal came a month after they had officially moved in together. Helen and Aiden had spent a rare free weekend at a music festival in the Midlands with mutual friends and had been travelling in the car back to Liverpool. Without any sort of build up (they had just finished talking about how much they both hated having to leave the festival so much earlier than their friends) Aiden said: 'You know what, Richards? You make me really happy. I think we should get hitched.'

Without a single moment's hesitation Helen surprised herself by saying: 'You know what, Reid? I've been sort of thinking the same thing myself.'

The plans for the wedding took on a life of their own and it seemed like every spare moment was taken up with making decisions about the logistics of various wedding venues and caterers and above all how best to curb the number of invitees without causing huge swathes of distant family and long lost friends irreparable offence. For Helen at the end of a long day at work, all this planning was exhausting and exasperating but she did it because she knew it would be worth it in order to create the perfect happy ending.

The first sign that things weren't quite going to plan came some six months after the proposal when Aiden came home from work one evening and informed her that he had been offered a job hosting an early evening music show for a BBC station in London.

'How could you do this?' yelled Helen who hadn't even been aware that he had put together a showreel let alone that he had been actively auditioning for jobs outside of Liverpool. 'We both agreed that we'd only ever look for jobs in the north-west.'

'I know,' replied Aiden. 'Which is exactly the reason why I didn't tell you. I never thought for a minute that I'd get the gig, but they loved me, Helen, they really loved me.'

Aiden explained his actions away in the same manner that he always explained everything away when people didn't agree with his methods, utilising a heady mixture of charm and bombast that enticed the listener into believing that to stand in his way was in effect to stand in the way of progress. 'It'll be the best thing that's ever happened to us,' he assured her. 'I've got a feeling, Helen, a really good feeling that this will be the making of both our careers.'

'And what about the wedding?' asked Helen. 'Do you want to call it off?'

'Of course I don't,' he replied. 'It's only a six-month contract. And I promise I'll be home every weekend and we can do all the wedding stuff you like. But this is a chance of a lifetime! My own show! Who knows what it might lead to. It's just too good to turn down.'

Although she wasn't entirely sure what Aiden's move would mean for them (after all her job, home and the majority of her close friends were in Liverpool), Helen knew that she couldn't stand in his way and so, despite her reservations, gave her blessing reciting to all who questioned her judgement the very arguments Aiden had used to convince her.

For the first few months while Aiden was away Helen kept herself busy with work and the wedding, choosing to live only for the weekends when Aiden would return from London. But when his show began to take off and his initial six-month contract was extended indefinitely Helen found herself becoming less patient and more enraged until finally one evening during a telephone

10

call he told her that he wouldn't be able to make it up at the weekend because he was too tired.

'Too tired?' repeated Helen indignantly. 'Have you any idea how tired I am? I work too! And I run this home and I'm planning this whole wedding by myself! How dare you tell me you're too tired to see me!'

Following the argument that ensued they didn't speak for two whole weeks but even through the worst of it Helen continued to work on the wedding plans convinced that all would be fine. And it was, inasmuch as, unable to cope without him, she travelled to London, apologised for the part she had played in the argument and promised to be more supportive of his career in the future. Everything returned to normal, which is to say that for Aiden at least not a single thing changed.

A week before the wedding Helen gathered together a group of her oldest, closest friends that had of course included Yaz, who was then working in marketing for a media company in Manchester, to a bar in Liverpool where they sipped cocktails and exchanged horror stories from their dating pasts, before moving on to a trendy restaurant near the quayside where well presented food was consumed and more cocktails imbibed before heading off to a nearby nightclub to dance until the early hours.

As daylight broke across Merseyside and Helen along with Yaz and a couple of other friends who were staying with her for the weekend returned to her apartment, Helen's phone rang.

'Is this Helen?' It was a female voice, young,

undeniably sexy even though currently laced with stress. Helen confirmed her identity. 'I think you should know that Aiden's been cheating on you.' Helen couldn't speak. The woman carried on regardless. 'He's a bastard, an absolute bastard and he doesn't deserve to be happy.'

Any doubts as to the veracity of this life-shattering statement evaporated when Aiden called her less than a minute later. He lied of course, claiming she was the deranged ex-girlfriend of a mate and was trying to get back at her ex by being a right royal pain in the arse to all around her, but Helen didn't buy it for a second. It wasn't the words so much as the guilt in Aiden's voice, which he seemed unable to hide almost as if on some unconscious level he actually wanted her to know the truth that he was too cowardly to say to her face.

Eventually forced to confess, Aiden blamed every-thing from the pressure of work to Helen's desire to stay in Liverpool for leading him astray, while Helen only blamed herself. As she contemplated the misery and embarrassment that lay before her she made two promises to herself: that she would never let her career backslide again for the sake of a man, and that if she fell in love again (which she couldn't imagine) she would never, absolutely never, agree to get married.

Leaving the indignities involved in having to cancel the wedding a week before it was due to her mum and Yaz, Helen managed to talk the travel agents where she had booked her honeymoon into allowing her to exchange it for eight nights at a spa hotel in Paxos, where she embarked on a daily routine of beauty treatments, sunbathing, swimming and drinking bottle after bottle of local wine to the point of unconsciousness.

Returning home she cleared out anything that reminded her of Aiden, gave up alcohol, took up running and buried herself in her job, thinking nothing of working weekends and double shifts. Helen soon attracted the attention of upper management and received a promotion to producer of the mid-morning current affairs show, a post which she'd had her eye on since joining the station. Although thrilled to have reached her goal within weeks of starting the job, she found it still wasn't quite enough. She wanted a bigger, better challenge, something that could completely absorb her and which she could mould as her own. It was only when she made these comments to Yaz late one Saturday evening when her friend had come to visit for the weekend that she finally realised what she wanted to be. 'I want to be on air,' she told Yaz, 'I want to be a presenter on my own show.'

Determined to make a point to whomever might care to observe it Helen devoted all her spare time to putting together an amazing showreel that highlighted both her natural skills as a broadcaster and those she had picked up working with the brightest and best at the various stations across the nation. On a sunny spring morning a few weeks later she crossed her fingers and sent the CDs she had prepared out to the ten best radio stations in the country.

Within six months every one of them had rejected her.

Refusing to give up, she continued sending out showreels until she had exhausted every option bar one.

Disheartened, she knocked on the office door of her own station manager and after a brief conversation outlining her desires had handed him the CD convinced that as well as marking the end of her dreams it would also result in the erosion of any credibility that she had. Management were suspicious of production people who wanted to become on-air talent: they felt it showed a lack of commitment while revealing the full extent of their bloated egos.

The following afternoon Helen got a call from the station manager's PA asking her to come and see him. Prepared for the worst Helen found herself nervously reviewing the job ads at the back of *Broadcast* as she waited to be called in to his office. When he told her that he had liked her showreel so much that he was offering her a try out covering Kit Emmerly's weekend overnight show the following month Helen convinced herself it was all an elaborate joke. It was only when she found herself covering Matthew Hutcherson's early-evening phone-in the month after, and Jane Edwards' mid-morning talkback show the month after that, that she finally accepted her dream was coming true right before her eyes. The day that they told her she had finally landed her own show, *Call-back, with Helen Richards*, an overnight show covering Monday to Thursday, she was on such a high that she didn't come down for days.

It was around this time, with a new job and the

worst of what had been a monstrously unhappy year behind her, that Yaz chose to announce that she and Simon were getting married. And it was at her friend's hastily thrown together engagement party that Helen encountered Phil Hudson for the first time and came to realise that the second of her vows made after splitting up with Aiden, might not be quite so easy to keep as the first.

2.

Meeting a potential life partner hadn't even been on Helen's agenda as she entered Simon and Yaz's crowded living room clutching a plastic cup of red wine. She hoped to chew over old times with a few good friends and at worst she thought she might drink too much, talk about work a little too loudly and around midnight end up dancing and singing to *I'm Every Woman*. It was, then, very much to her surprise, when after three glasses of wine and an hour of room circulating she found herself being introduced to Phil, one of Simon's friends, and thinking as his hand touched hers: "Hmm, he's nice."

Phil was tall but not too tall. He had short black hair, dark brown eyes that seemed to radiate warmth and peeking out from underneath his hairline by his right temple was a tiny scar. He was wearing jeans and a long-sleeved black t-shirt, which was so tight across the shoulders that Helen was tempted to reach out and give the outline of each deltoid a prod with her index finger.

'Are you okay?'

Helen blinked, aware that she had been away in her

own private daydream. 'Yes, yes. Sorry about that. I was away with the fairies.'

'No problem,' said Phil. 'I just wanted to make sure that you weren't drifting off into a diabetic coma. That would have been terrible.'

'For me or for you?'

Phil was horrified. 'You're not actually diabetic are you?'

Helen shook her head and Phil wiped imaginary sweat from his brow.

'I thought I'd really put my foot in it there.'

'Don't worry, there's still plenty of time.'

They continued talking, mainly about Simon and Yaz. Phil thought Yaz was the best thing that had ever happened to Simon and liked the way that she seemed to have calmed down the excesses of his youth. He usually saw them two or three times a year but wished he could see them more because although he had friends where he lived, none were as good as Simon.

Phil revealed that he was the owner of Sharper Sounds, a high end TV and hi-fi shop in Derby. Helen deliberately played down her job's glamorous side and focused on the hard work that she had to put in every day but she couldn't help feeling a flush of pride when he appeared genuinely impressed, even asking her to send him a CD of her show to listen to in the car on his way to work. She took his address and promised that she would send him the disc first thing Monday morning, but even as she kissed him on the cheek as they parted, she knew it wasn't going to happen. Nice as he seemed she wasn't anywhere near ready to start dating again.

The next time they met was the following New Year's Eve when Simon and Yaz had a small get-together at their house. Phil and several of Simon's other friends arrived just after seven and the first thing Phil did on seeing Helen was to ask her what happened to the recording she had promised to send. Helen had lied and blamed the post, but Phil said that it didn't matter anyway as he had offered one of his regular mail-order customers a ten per cent discount if they sent him a recording of her show. He claimed to have listened to it so many times that he had inadvertently committed parts to memory and proceeded to recite a minute's worth of on-air banter about women's underwear that she had exchanged with Sandy, the weather girl following the three o'clock news. Phil's teasing had Helen in stitches and for the rest of the evening all they did was talk and laugh.

'Call me and we'll meet up,' she said as she hurriedly tapped her home number into his phone.

'Promise?'

'On my life.'

Two days later, as she sat on her sofa watching TV Phil did indeed call but she didn't pick up. Instead she stood next to the machine while he left a long and rambling message in the style of Sandy, the weather girl. The message made her laugh out loud but it also had the effect of making her think about the past, and she shed more tears in a single evening than she had in the previous six months.

Finally, some six months later, they met for a third time, on Simon and Yaz's wedding day, in their roles as best man and maid of honour. At the reception, as Simon and Yaz took to the floor for the first dance of the evening Phil turned to Helen and asked her what exactly she was afraid of and without missing a beat she said: 'Getting hurt, again.'

He gave her words careful consideration then reached for her hand and squeezed it, as if he was confident that this small action was all the reassurance she could need. In any other man, Helen would have found this response remarkable in its inadequacy but from Phil it felt like a beautifully eloquent gesture. He made her feel safe, he made her feel cherished and right there and then she knew he was all that she wanted.

Nine years, two house moves, three job changes, a large mortgage and a red setter called Samson later and Helen felt exactly the same way. Phil made her feel safe and secure and they were happy, really happy, until one evening out in the centre of Nottingham enjoying a post-cinema visit to Nando's, Phil went and spoilt it all.

'Look what I've found,' he said reaching down beneath their table. He held out his hand and showed Helen a bright pink plastic ring with a red plastic jewel in the middle.

'Somewhere out there is an under-accessorised

four-year-old who is ruining her poor mum's evening because she's lost her favourite ring,' joked Helen. 'You should hand it in to the staff, there might even be a reward.'

'Or,' mused Phil, 'I could just give it to you.'

Helen stared at the ring, saying nothing.

She was obviously in need of greater encouragement. He rolled the ring between his thumb and forefinger. 'So come on then. How about it?'

She pushed his hand away. 'Very funny, Hudson, you've had your fun, that's enough.'

Defiantly, Phil placed the ring on the table in front of his plate. 'Plenty of men would be more than a little bit crushed by a comment like that.'

'Well given that you're not one of them the point is, as they say, moot. Now, eat up and tell me what you thought of the film. If you're lucky I might even pass off a few of your more perceptive comments as my own in tomorrow's show when Carol-the-film-critic comes in for her slot.'

Phil began sawing at the chicken leg in front of him in a petulant fashion while Helen breathed a sigh of relief. She took a bite of her chicken burger and looked at Phil expecting to see him chewing. His lips were set in a grim line.

Helen calmly set down her burger.

'What now?'

'Is there any need to use that voice?'

'What voice?'

'Your annoyed voice.'

'I am annoyed, Phil! I just wanted us to have a nice night out and now you're being all weird and sulky for no reason.'

'No reason?' Phil snorted loudly. 'Of course there's a reason! I can't believe that you still don't get it!'

'Get what?'

'How insulting it is.'

'How insulting what is? I have no idea what you're talking about!'

Phil's eyes widened in disbelief. 'Are you kidding? I've just asked you to marry me!'

'Using a kid's toy ring that you found on the floor! Am I supposed to be flattered?'

'You know that's not the point! I'm always asking you to marry me, and you're always saying the same thing. How many times do I have to ask before you say yes?'

Hearing the genuine hurt in his voice amongst the anger and indignation made Helen feel terrible. He was right, of course. She had lost count of the number of times he had proposed. There had been several formal proposals in their first three years (one in a Michelin-starred restaurant on their first anniversary, another, in Venice during a private gondola ride as they passed under the Rialto Bridge) followed by countless informal ones over the next seven years when he was bored, drunk, sober, amorous, sentimental and, on at least one occasion, angry. No matter the context or the manner in which the question was posed Helen's response had always been the same.

21

'What do we need to get married for when things are working just fine as they are?' asked Helen wearily.

'Do you have that on a recording?' Phil said bitterly. 'Because you really ought to. Could you imagine? With a single press of a button on your iPhone your response – downloaded directly from completecliches.com – would be played back to any unsuspecting man who dared to suggest spending the rest of his life with you.'

'But I do want to spend the rest of my life with you, you must know that by now. I'm not going anywhere, Phil. I've got a mortgage with you, I've got Samson with you, in fact I've pretty much built my life around you. Isn't that enough?'

'If it was I wouldn't be asking you, would I?'

'And that's it is it? You want so you get? I just don't want to get married and I don't understand why you won't respect that.'

'You know why.'

Helen sighed. 'What would you say if I told you I didn't?'

'I'd tell you that – deliberately or otherwise – you were lying. You know as well as I do that this is all about him. It always has been and it always will be.' He stood up, his face revealing the same blend of hurt and anger as his voice. 'I'll see you at home. For some reason I've completely lost my appetite.'

Phil was wrong. She was sure of this. Not wanting to get married had nothing to do with Aiden. Aiden was just an ex. A part of her history that she would have willingly erased from her brain years ago. As it was, he

was a part of her history that few would let her forget
because rather than disappearing without a trace after
his initial success in London as Helen had hoped,
professionally Aiden had gone the opposite way,
rocketing to the top of the radio and TV talent pool.
The man who had been so broke when they first met
that he'd had to borrow money from her to take her
out on their first date was now a multi-millionaire radio
and TV presenter, with (if the tabloids were to be
believed) a pop star for an ex-wife and a string of
glamorous model girlfriends to help ease the pain of
life at the top.

Since Aiden's rise to fame Helen had lost count of
the times tabloid hacks looking for an angle on a story
about Aiden had dug up her name from his cuttings file
and either doorstepped her in the hope of getting a
reaction to whatever newsworthy antics he had been
up to or offered her hard cash for an exclusive, private
photos of the two of them together, plus studio shots
of her wearing 'something sexy' to illustrate the story.
Helen ignored the offers and the journalists themselves,
in the hope that they would go away but she had naïvely
believed that her former fiancé's fame and fortune
hadn't impacted at all on her relationship with Phil.

It was some time after ten when Helen got home to the
three-storey Victorian terrace in Beeston which she
shared with Phil.

She hung up her jacket, kicked off her shoes and
called out to Phil over the sound of the TV coming

from the living room. He didn't respond, which Helen thought was stupid and childish but also possibly an indicator of just how strongly he felt about this issue.

Phil was sitting in the leather armchair in the corner of the room staring grimly at the TV. He looked over, his face as unfamiliar and unyielding as it had been in the restaurant, picked up the remote and switched off the set, a sign that he was attempting to meet her halfway.

She sat down on the sofa opposite.

'Did you really mean what you said earlier?'

'Forget it. I was blowing off steam that's all. I'm sorry, okay.'

'I can't forget it though, can I? You know I love you, I love you more than anything or anyone. And what you said really hurt.'

He looked down at the stripped oak floor. 'Then I'm sorry. I was out of line. Look, just forget I said anything.' He pointed to the TV with the remote. 'I was just watching the tail end of that Denzel Washington film you like. Why don't you make yourself a cup of tea and come and sit with me for a while?'

Helen didn't move. 'It's not because of him you know. It's got nothing to do with him at all.'

Phil smiled wryly. 'Who? Denzel? I'm glad to hear it because I don't think I'd stand a chance against a guy like that.'

Relieved that Phil was back to making stupid jokes rather than being angry with her, Helen went to sit at his feet and rested her head on his knees.

He stroked her hair. 'I shouldn't have rocked the boat like that. You're right, we don't need to make any changes.'

'But that's not true, is it?' said Helen looking up at him. 'This keeps coming up and it's not fair on you. I need you to believe that it was never about him. It was always – absolutely always – about me thinking that good things go bad when you try and change them.'

'Look, you've got to remember that I'm this ordinary guy with a rubbish education who happens to have got lucky with you. Meanwhile the bloke who broke your heart just happens to be a ridiculously good-looking, well-educated millionaire TV presenter who can snap his fingers and have any woman he wants. How am I supposed to compete with that?'

Helen took both his hands in hers and kissed them. 'You have no idea how amazing you are, do you? You're twice the man he'll ever be.'

'Look,' said Phil, 'the point is I've always felt like the whole marriage thing is off the cards because of him. He hurt you, I get it, he let you down, but I'm not him.'

'I never said you were.'

'You didn't need to. He's been hanging around us since day one.'

'That's not true.'

Phil raised an eyebrow. 'So the reason you never called me when we first met was nothing to do with him?' Helen didn't reply. 'Look,' continued Phil, 'I'm not having a go, I promise you. All I'm saying is that I want the mistakes I get blamed for to be mine and mine alone. That's not too much to ask, is it?'

Tears began to roll down Helen's cheeks. 'I'm sorry, Phil, I'm really sorry.'

'It's fine. I just wanted to get that off my chest and now I promise I'll never ask you to marry me again.'

'Good,' said Helen, 'because it's about time I took my turn.'

3.

Helen was struggling on the stairs with the 'slightly larger' suitcase she had eventually chosen when her phone rang. Being in danger of being crushed to death if she attempted to leave it precariously propped up against the banisters while she took the call she soldiered on and after a great deal of time, low volume expletives and exertion she succeeded in her task. She looked at the screen and saw that the missed call was from her mum. Closing her eyes she drew a deep breath and pressed the call button.

'Hi, Mum how are you?'

'I'm ever so good thank you, sweetie. You're not on the motorway are you? You know you shouldn't take calls and drive don't you?'

Helen laughed. 'No, I'm not driving – I haven't even left yet! Yaz is coming for me any minute.'

'Are you excited? That picture you showed me of the hotel the other day looked ever so lovely.'

'I can't wait, Mum. It's easily the poshest place I'll ever stay in.'

'Well you deserve it. You work so hard it's a wonder you haven't keeled over with exhaustion. Is Phil still there?'

'He went this morning. Yaz's husband picked him up.'

'Where have they gone again?'

'Amsterdam.'

'I hope he's not doing anything bad while he's there. You do read such stories about the things young men get up to on these stag weekends. There was a programme on cable the other day – I only saw it as I was flicking through – there was a group of lads sitting outside a bar and one of them kept dropping his trousers and the camera had to go all funny so that you couldn't see his backside.'

Helen just managed to stop herself laughing. 'I promise you, Mum, Phil will definitely not be dropping his trousers in public. He's not that kind of guy. In fact my weekend will probably end up more raucous than his.'

'I don't know why you young people need to have these stag and hen things. Your father and I didn't and we were none the worse for it.'

Helen swallowed. 'How is Dad?'

'Exactly the same. Nothing changes.'

'He seemed brighter last time I visited him. Much more like his old self.'

'I doubt that.'

'You have to keep positive, Mum.'

'And keep lying to myself like you do? He's not going to be well enough to walk you down the aisle, Helen, it's just not going to happen. Your dad's ill and that's all there is to it, and he'll get worse and worse until one day if we're lucky his body will give way just like his mind did and put him out of his misery. It's a terrible thing to see a proud man like your father in this state.'

They continued talking out of mutual feelings of guilt rather than the desire to communicate and once their time was served they prepared to exchange civil goodbyes.

'Okay, Mum,' said Helen. 'I'd better go as Yaz will be here soon. I'll see you later.'

'Yes of course,' replied her mum. 'But just a quickie before you go . . . about the wedding dress.'

'Mum, I've already said that I'm not talking about it.'

'I know you did and I still don't know why. Your auntie Caron was asking about it only last night. Have you any idea how embarrassing it is for me to have to say that I haven't seen a picture of it!'

'No one has, Mum, I told you, this is something I want to do on my own. I don't understand why you won't respect that.'

There was a click and the line went dead. Helen filled with rage. Why did her mum always insist on winding her up like this? Why did she always insist on getting her own way?

Much as they loved each other (and they did, quite fiercely) their outlook on life differed too much for them to have any common ground when it came to how Helen should live her life.

Despite Helen having explained her desire to do things differently this time around her mum seemed incapable of accepting this fact but it was the topic of

Helen's father that caused the most upset between them. (Her mum, a practitioner of the school of thought that called a spade a spade, viewed her husband's rapid descent into the advanced stages of Alzheimer's almost as if he had already died while Helen, an eternal optimist at least in terms of her father's health, refused to even consider that a day might come when her father would be permanently absent from her life.)

Helen headed upstairs to get the rest of her bags and, when the doorbell rang, she checked her reflection in the mirror and opened the door to an impatient-looking Yaz, holding a carrier bag.

Helen opened the door wider for Yaz to step in. 'Before you start, I know what you said about not going overboard with the luggage . . .' Her voice trailed off as she pointed to the bulging case and numerous bags standing in the middle of the hallway. 'I tried to keep it to a minimum but I failed, okay? So, don't give me a hard time about it.'

Yaz stared in disbelief. 'How long do you think we're going for? Is there anything you haven't packed? If I open up that case will I find you've brought the kitchen sink?'

'Look, do you want me to have a good time or not?'

'Of course I do! But I was sort of hoping that you'd be able to do it without bringing your entire wardrobe. Is everything in there absolutely necessary?'

Helen shrugged. 'I don't know, but it's too late to try editing it now. It took me the best part of ten minutes to get it closed so I'm not risking opening it again until we get there.'

Yaz rolled her eyes theatrically. 'Okay, fine, you take the case. It's not like the rest of the girls will need to sit down or anything. But you have to do something for me.' She reached into the carrier bag and pulled out a bright pink T-shirt with a photo of Helen taken on her last birthday wearing a three-cocktail grin and a pink glittery cowboy hat with the words 'Bride in training' emblazoned across it. Helen had never seen anything quite so ugly in her life.

'No!'

'But you have to!'

'Why?'

'Because it'll be fun.'

'But you promised we weren't going to do this kind of stuff. You said – and I quote: "The weekend will be tasteful," which means no male strippers, no inflatable willies and no tacky T-shirts!'

'And it will be tasteful. Just not this bit. Come on, mate, indulge me this once.'

Feeling guilty about the suitcase, Helen reluctantly accepted the offending items. She slipped the T-shirt gingerly over her top, placed the hat on her head and stared at her reflection in the hallway mirror.

'I look like an idiot.'

'True,' said Yaz practically speechless with laughter, 'but you won't be alone.' She put on her own T-shirt and hat, pulled a camera out of her bag and took a photo of Helen. 'There,' she said, checking the photo on her camera's tiny screen, 'if that isn't one for your Facebook page I don't know what is!'

Helen wondered how she might have spent this weekend had she not succumbed to the pressure to have a hen do. Although she was looking forward to The Manor, with a week to go before the wedding and so many unchecked items on her to-do list, the thought of it all made her feel as though she was drowning in a sea of uncompleted tasks.

From the moment Helen confessed to her friends and co-workers that she and Phil were finally getting married, the question of the hen night became paramount. Given the disaster of her previous hen night, Helen had been keen to forgo the tradition completely, but every time she attempted to explain her stance to those around her she received the same 'I don't get it' blank stare. 'It's because most of us are in our late thirties and haven't been to a hen party for years,' explained Yaz, when Helen commented on her friends' reaction, 'and if anyone's in need of an excuse to let down their hair and blow off some steam it's got to be our demographic all the way. This isn't just about you H, it's about them. Your friends need a hen do.'

Although Yaz's tongue was lodged firmly in her cheek throughout much of this speech, Helen conceded she had a point. Lots of her friends who were married – with or without kids – would love to have some time to themselves without having to feel guilty. Relenting, Helen handed Yaz a list of the people she wanted to invite and gave the go ahead for what she hoped might be a modest get-together at a local posh pizza place in West Bridgford, followed by an evening of cocktails and dancing. One week and several phone calls later those plans had morphed into a two-night stay at a five-star luxury hotel on the edge of the Peak District.

'I know I'm being a right bossy old cow,' said Yaz as the two friends made their way into the kitchen, 'but it's only because I want you to have the most amazing weekend, babe.'

'I know it is,' said Helen hugging her friend, 'And while I might not always look like I appreciate all the effort you've put in I really do. It can't have been easy sorting all this out while juggling the kids.'

Helen sat down at the kitchen counter idly flicking through a magazine while Yaz went to the loo. Then she washed up a dirty plate and mug, turned on the burglar alarm and locked the front door. With great effort the two women managed to drag Helen's luggage to Yaz's dark blue people carrier aka The Mum-mobile and loaded it in the rear of the vehicle.

'Right,' said Yaz starting up the engine as Helen buckled her seatbelt, 'I've got the bride to be and her extensive luggage now all I need to do is pick up the girls and this weekend has officially begun!'

'The girls', to be accurate, were three women, Lorna, Dee and Kerry, who formed the inner core of Helen's friends. Helen had known Scottish-born-and-raised Lorna since first moving to Nottingham when she had been an overworked and underpaid stylist at one of the city's coolest hair salons and the only woman who

Helen would let within an inch of her hair. Back then Lorna was constantly broke and had a serious unsuitable boyfriend addiction. Now she was still the only woman Helen would allow to cut her hair but she was also solvent and happily co-habiting with Dez, her boyfriend of three years. She was also the owner/manager of Revival, an up-market salon in the centre of Beeston catering to the great and the good of its well-heeled constituency.

Next there was Dee, a previous next-door neighbour, a big-hearted, plus-sized, Abba-loving ball of energy and English teacher. Dee and her husband Johnny had been the couple that Helen and Phil socialised with most after Yaz and Simon. Then Johnny left and everything changed. Now single, Dee worked for a Nottingham-based adult education outreach agency and when not going on teeth-grindingly awful internet dates her favourite thing was to regale Helen with tales of teeth-grindingly awful internet dates.

Finally, there was twenty-six-year-old Kerry, the baby of the group, whom Helen had known since Kerry's first day at Radio Sherwood as a single, timid, fresh out of university trainee broadcast assistant. Seeing more of herself in Kerry than she liked to admit, Helen had taken her under her nurturing wing. Five years on and recently engaged, Kerry had worked her way up the ranks to become the producer of Helen's revamped afternoon show and had done such a brilliant job that the show had been nominated for its first ever Sony Award.

Although Helen saw the girls individually, they also met

up every couple of months for a seemingly innocent meal which would inevitably morph – several drinks in – into the kind of evening that required a frenzied exchange of phone calls the following day to piece together exactly what had happened.

'What's taken you so long?' exclaimed Dee wrenching open Kerry's front door before Helen had finished making her way up the path. 'Somewhere out there is a swanky room with my name on it that's going to waste while we sit watching daytime TV!'

Helen hugged her friend tightly with one hand while holding on to her hat with the other. 'Rest assured Yaz will have her foot to the floor the whole way. No one wants to be at that hotel faster than she does. That's why she refused to let me drive.'

Dee wrinkled her nose. 'That's because you drive like my Nan! In fact scrap that, you actually drive worse than her because bless her, while she's convinced that if she goes over forty she'll end up in outer space, at least I have seen her do thirty-one in a thirty-zone on a couple of occasions.'

'I'm a law-abiding citizen!' protested Helen.

'More like a law-abiding *senior* citizen!'

Realising that it was highly unlikely that she would ever win this argument, Helen changed the subject.

'Yaz is going to go bonkers when she sees that lot!' said Helen pointing at the mass of weekend bags, miniature suitcases and designer logoed carrier bags at her friends' feet. 'She gave me a hard time and it's my hen-do!'

'What's your hen do?'

Yaz, who had been making room for the girls' luggage in the car, was standing in the doorway wearing a quizzical expression on her face and holding the carrier bag containing the pink hats and T-shirts.

'Nothing,' said Helen. She shuffled next to Kerry and Lorna in the hope of hiding the bags from view. 'We were just chatting.'

'Why are you all yakking instead of getting the weekend started? Is this how it's going to be? Me organising and you lot goofing off all the time?'

'You love it really.'

'Well,' said Yaz, 'That's as maybe but it doesn't mean you have to take advantage of my good nature.' She handed out the hats and T-shirts. 'Before you start moaning like this one did, you don't have to wear them all weekend but they are compulsory in the car *at all times*.'

'She's not joking,' said Helen, 'my hat fell off on the way over and she pulled over and waited until I'd put it back on.'

'I know it all sounds a bit draconian,' said Yaz, 'but you'll thank me once the weekend's over and all you have is memories.'

Lorna laughed, 'Is that an actual command or are we allowed to thank you of our own free will?'

'She doesn't care as long as we do,' said Kerry fluttering her eyelashes sweetly.

The girls put on the T-shirts and hats while Yaz, as predicted, told them off for over-packing. It took the best part of half an hour to pack all the luggage into Yaz's people carrier and even then there were multiple handbags and carrier bags left which in the end Dee, Kerry and Lorna had to have on their laps as punishment.

Soon after loading up they were slipping *Never Forget: The Ultimate Take That Collection* into the CD player and journeying their way towards the A52, belting out the lyrics to *A Million Love Songs* at the tops of their voices and feeling like they didn't have a care in the world.

4.

The blazing summer sun was high in the sky as Yaz slowed the car and pulled in between the grand limestone pillars at the entrance to The Manor. Reaching for the dashboard she turned down the volume of the music that had accompanied them for the entire journey to a bare minimum and wound down her window to take in the unmistakable sounds and smells of the English countryside – Beeston, this was not.

'Hey, Yaz!' called Helen as she too wound down her window, 'this place is so up-market that even the Mum-mobile crunching on the gravel sounds classy. If I close my eyes I can almost imagine we're in a Rolls-Royce heading up to our country pile for the weekend.'

The driveway was long and winding, not only to make the most of the surrounding countryside but also to heighten the anticipation of arrival and it did both extremely well. Straining to get the first peek at the place that would soon be home, Helen and the girls were literally on the edge of their seats until round a sharp bend there it was: a beautifully constructed, architecturally imposing, white stone country house looking out over a wide shimmering reed-lined river.

'Now *that*,' said Yaz, 'is what I call a hotel!' She turned to Helen. 'What do you think then? Still wishing we'd stayed at home?'

'It's amazing,' said Helen as the drive swept over a bridge and up towards the house. 'Come check-out time on Sunday they are literally going to have to prise me kicking and screaming from my room.'

'This is going to be one of the best weekends of my life,' said Helen as they came to a halt at the main entrance and a young man, in a dark grey shirt and trousers, handsome enough to be a model, descended the stairs. 'It's too perfect for words.'

The porter greeted Helen and her friends warmly and pointed them in the direction of reception while he began unloading the luggage. Not needing to be told twice, the girls made their way to the reception desk where they were welcomed by a pretty French girl, also dressed in the hotel's dark grey uniform. She allocated their rooms, handing out slim, black key cards inside stiff white card wallets. None of the rooms had numbers, instead they were all named after the different types of trees that could be found in the hotel grounds. Yaz's was called Bird Cherry, Lorna's was Larch, Dee's Chestnut, Kerry's Bay Willow and Helen's the Sycamore room.

'Right then,' said Yaz, after the receptionist had given them directions to all the rooms, 'according to my schedule it's free time from now until seven thirty when we'll meet in the Silver Lounge, for cocktails.' Stifling her competing desires to both mock and hug

39

Yaz for having made a schedule, Helen made her way to the lift.

Despite having spent many idle moments in her studio poring over the artfully fashioned photos on the hotel website, Helen was astonished by how much better the reality was than its two-dimensional counterpart. As she stood in the doorway to her new home for the next two nights she could hardly believe her eyes. There were glossy magazines on the Danish coffee table in the lounge area, a beautifully presented bouquet of freshly cut flowers on the dressing table, and a small box of handcrafted Belgian chocolates on the bed. And as for the room itself, everything from the antique French chandelier to the vintage satin cream duvet cover resplendent across the super-king-sized bed, from the state of the art Bang and Olufsen TV through to the Ligne Roset floor lamp screamed luxury to such an extent that Helen wondered if she had slipped into the pages of *Elle Decoration*.

As a rule Helen's favourite part of any posh hotel experience was the bathroom. Yes, she appreciated tastefully chosen furnishings, and attention-grabbing colour palettes but nothing quite got her going like an exquisitely decorated bathroom and so it was with no small degree of trepidation that she approached the only door in the room she had yet to open.

She was not disappointed. It was perfect, absolutely perfect. Four times the size of her own bathroom, presented in a classic dove white and decked out with a twin sink, a zinc-floored walk-in shower with a huge rainfall showerhead, and a roll-top bath to die for. It was beyond her wildest bathroom imaginings.

But even so, as she unwrapped one of the individual rose petal soaps she observed that without the sound of Phil in the other room, flicking through the TV channels and bemoaning the price of a bottled beer from the mini-bar, she might as well have been in a fifty-pound-a-night Novotel. *Maybe that's what love means*, she thought as she began drawing herself a bath. *You can only be happy in paradise if the person you love is there with you to share it.'*

It was a little after six when a wet-haired Helen, encased in one of the hotel's super fluffy towelling robes and matching slippers emerged from the bathroom and opened up her case. Her excitement at the prospect of getting ready for the evening ahead was tempered by a slight feeling of stress. Having had barely any time to plan her outfits during the week, she had spent a frantic afternoon in Nottingham city centre purchasing half a dozen tops, two pairs of trousers and four different hair accessories, most of which she knew she would be returning unused first thing on Monday morning. In her work life Helen was the very definition of decisive but standing alone and faced with so many sartorial options she felt the complete opposite.

Deciding to leave her choice of clothes until later Helen picked up her hairdryer and as she did so there was a sharp knock at her door.

Helen's immediate thought revealed much about the negative nature of her psychology, for she assumed that the knock heralded the arrival of a member of the hotel's staff to tell her there had been a hideous mix-up and that she would have to leave her room immediately and stay in a nearby bed and breakfast. When she opened the door to see Yaz, Lorna, Dee and Kerry brandishing a condensation-covered bottle of Cava, and carrying piles of clothes, shoes, and make-up bags, she was both relieved and cheered.

'It was all her idea,' said Yaz pointing at Dee.

'And I'm not ashamed of it either!' grinned Dee, as unbidden the girls all made their way into Helen's room and closed the door behind them. 'Getting ready for a big night out is the best part of an evening!' Her face fell. 'You don't mind, do you?'

'Mind?' said Helen, 'I've never been so bloody grateful to see you lot in my life! Dee you open the Cava, Lorna you find some glasses, Kerry, put some music on, Yaz, well . . . you can just make yourself at home and I am going to blow-dry my hair into submission, then with your help throw together a killer outfit, paint my face to within an inch of its life and leave this room for dinner tonight looking like a million dollars!'

The hour and a half that followed was like a montage from a chick flick. Not just any chick flick montage. The ultimate chick flick montage with the best bits from *Dirty Dancing*, *Thelma and Louise*, *Beaches* and *Mamma Mia* with all the associated tears, laughter, lip-syncing dance sequences and gratuitous displays of female bonding that such a description implies. And at the end of it all as Helen admired herself in the mirrored wardrobe in her new sleeveless embroidered black top, skinny leg trousers and black heels, standing next to her impeccably dressed and beautifully made-up friends as the final chorus of *Relight My Fire* played loudly from the wall mounted stereo system, she knew it would be a night to remember.

The five friends were still laughing and joking with each other when they emerged from the lift and clicked their way across the marble tiled lobby until they reached the Silver Lounge.

Again the Manor website photographs didn't do justice to the true opulence and sophistication of the Silver Lounge. Perfectly air-conditioned, with walls alternately painted in a gun-metal grey and brilliant white, furnished with sumptuous velvet sofas arranged around low gloss white tables and with lighting so subdued that even seven thirty on a summer's evening could have passed for three in the morning, it was every inch the perfect place for the five friends to start their evening.

Spreading themselves across two of the huge velvet sofas the girls pored over the cocktail menu before jointly making the decision that they would each order something different. Drinks orders were taken and then taken again because half the group had changed their minds before the waiter had even left their table and then the girls settled into a quarter of an hour of gentle banter before their drinks and several small platters of olives and nuts were presented to them.

'We should have a toast,' said Kerry raising her glass. 'Here's to our girl Helen, one of the best friends a girl could have!'

Clinking glasses, the girls ploughed headlong into more laughter and conversation while exchanging sips of cocktails with each other along the way. This resulted with almost indecent haste in a table full of empty glasses and a call to the waiter for the return of the drinks menu. He arrived to the eruption of a cacophony of screaming and laughter that could only mean one thing: more of Helen's weekend hen party guests had arrived.

The three new arrivals were friends who for one reason or another (most often a clash of schedules) Helen rarely got to see. There was Dublin-born Ros, a tall and elegant Cambridge-based former magazine journalist turned web-developer who was currently in the middle of a divorce. Then there was Heather, a Bournemouth-based former paediatric nurse now a happily married full-time mum of four who Helen knew from her sixth-form days. Finally there was Carla, a part-time social worker and single mum of two who she'd known since they both started Brownies together at the age of eight and with whom she had recently reconnected via Facebook after a fifteen-year gap.

Helen raced over to the girls, hugged them and ushered them over to the sofas to be introduced to the rest of the party.

'Everyone,' said Helen eagerly, 'this is Ros, Heather and Carla.' The girls all waved their hellos. 'Ros, Heather and Carla, meet the girls!'

As she caught up with everyone's news Helen remembered the reservations she had had about the weekend. Surrounded by some of her oldest and closest friends, watching them all laughing and joking together, it seemed impossible that she had entertained such thoughts. This weekend couldn't be more different from that raucous night in Liverpool all those years ago. More importantly, this time she wasn't marrying an egocentric idiot who would break her heart.

Tapping her engagement ring (a platinum four-claw mount with a single carat diamond ring that Phil had surprised her with the weekend after she proposed) on the side of her glass, Helen rose and called the girls to attention.

'I just wanted you all to know how much it means to me that you've come this weekend. We've all got such busy lives and hardly a scrap of time for ourselves, so the fact that you've all arranged baby-sitters, put off spending time with husbands and partners for the weekend just to be here means a tremendous amount to me. And, well, I think you're all amazing!'

A tearful Helen sat down while the girls all applauded, Yaz joking that secretly they had only come for the pampering, and as they raised a glass for yet another toast the waiter arrived to inform them that their table was ready.

'I know we've got lovely treatments and everything

booked for the weekend,' said Yaz, as the girls finished off their drinks and gathered their things, 'but do you think it's wrong for me to be looking forward to this meal most? I'm tingling with excitement at the prospect of a nice meal that I didn't cook!'

Herded by Yaz, the party made their way into a large modern dining room where various tables of diners were already eating. One of the waiting staff checked their reservation and showed them to their table, which Yaz noticed immediately was too small.

'I think there must have been a mistake. This is a table for six.'

The waiter nodded, returned to his station to pick up the reservation book and then consulted it in front of her.

'You are?'

'Mrs Collins.'

'And the number in your party is?'

'Eight.'

The waiter turned the book sideways to show Yaz what number was written down next to her name. There was no doubt about it. It was a six.

'But that can't be right! Yes, initially it was only going to be six tonight but then about three weeks ago I called and changed the number of guests to eight. Whoever took the call must have forgotten to change the booking.'

The waiter smiled apologetically. 'I'm so sorry about this Mrs Collins but I'm afraid I can only go with what's down in the book.'

Yaz looked as if she might explode. 'Okay, fine, can you at least find us another table?'

'I am afraid I can't do that madam as we are fully booked this evening.'

Helen stepped in. 'Okay, so we can't have another table. How about if we all squeeze up a bit? Do you think you could get in another couple of chairs and two extra settings?'

The waiter offered what Helen hoped would be his last conciliatory smile. 'I'm afraid, madam, that's not The Manor's dining policy. Might I suggest that you divide your group into two sittings?'

This suggestion was the final straw for Yaz. She glared at him and barked loudly enough to grab the attention of half the room: 'What a stupid idea! We're on a hen weekend, not a school trip! We're not going to eat in two sittings, we're going to eat all together at a table for eight because I don't care what's in that book of yours, that's what I asked for!'

Helen quickly put her arm around Yaz. 'Look, I'm really sorry. As you can see my friend's quite upset by all this. We'll just do the two sitting thing, okay?'

'No, we will not!' yelled Yaz. 'You all think that I've cocked up somehow, well I didn't! I booked a table for eight!'

'It's fine, babe, honestly,' said Helen quickly, 'No one blames you for anything.'

'But that's not the point!' snapped Yaz, 'The point is that I called and altered the booking three whole weeks ago and they told me there would be no problem and lo and behold there is one! It's just so typical! You do everything to have things planned out and through no fault of your own it all falls apart! I'm absolutely bloody sick of it!'

Yaz was always forceful but this was far from being her normal behaviour. Helen drew her aside. 'Listen, let's go outside and take a breather for five minutes.'

Yaz didn't reply. She pushed past the waiter and stormed out leaving Helen and at least half the dining room wondering what in the world was going on.

5.

Helen exchanged glances with the rest of the girls. There was something about the way Dee, Lorna and Kerry avoided her gaze that indicated they had more than an inkling of what was really going on.

'Okay, which one of you is going to tell me?'

Dee reluctantly met Helen's gaze. 'She made us promise not to say anything.'

'About what exactly? Has something happened?'

Dee's face fell and she bit her lip.

'She's fine and I'm sure you would have been the first person she told had the circumstances been different.'

'What circumstances?'

'The wedding. You getting married.'

'What's that got to do with her storming off like that?'

'Simon's moved out.'

Helen couldn't believe what she was hearing. 'No! When?'

'Three weeks ago.'

'Are you sure?'

Dee nodded. 'She told us all a few days ago but swore us to secrecy.'

'But that doesn't make any sense. Only this morning

49

she was telling me this long and involved story about how disorganised he was today getting his stuff together to pick up Phil. Why would she make that up?'

'Maybe she wanted to protect you,' said Lorna. 'Maybe she didn't want you worrying about her on what's supposed to be your special weekend.'

Helen's mouth felt dry and she wanted to sit down. 'Is he seeing someone else?'

Kerry shrugged. 'We don't know. She wouldn't give specifics. She talked about it like it was a trial separation so I'm guessing there's still hope.'

'A trial separation? Why would they do that? They're happy. I know they are. I've got to go and find her. I've got to find out exactly what's been going on.' She looked over at Lorna. 'I'm probably going to be a while and I'd hate for you girls to just be sitting around all night. Can you make sure that everyone gets fed and if there are any more problems . . . I don't know . . . order room service and get them to put it on my bill.'

Leaving them to smooth things over with the waiter Helen rushed out of the dining room and frantically scanned the lobby. Hazarding a guess Yaz might have gone for a cigarette she made her way outside and finally caught sight of her friend heading along the path to the river. Helen called out at the top of her voice drawing the attention of a number of people sitting out on the terrace but she didn't care what they thought of her. All she cared about was Yaz.

'You okay?' asked Helen when she finally caught up with her friend.

Without acknowledging her question Yaz gazed up at a flock of Canada geese flying overhead. 'This place really is amazing isn't it?' she said. 'How great would it be to wake up every morning and see this from your bedroom window?'

Helen put her arms around Yaz and held her tightly. 'It's perfect. You were so right when you chose here.'

Arm in arm they began walking along the river's edge and then out to the sun-bleached jetty where they stood watching the dying embers of the day's light dancing on the water's surface.

'The girls told you then,' said Yaz. She pulled out a lighter and a pack of Silk Cut, lit one up and took a long, deep pull on it then exhaled, sending a plume of smoke up into the air.

Helen nodded. 'Don't be mad at them. I practically had to drag it out of them.'

'I was going to tell you,' said Yaz, ' . . . it was just . . . I don't know . . . I really wanted this weekened to be special. I didn't want anything to spoil it. The last thing I wanted was to turn a weekend that was supposed to be all about you into a weekend that was all about me. I just wanted you to be happy.'

'And I will be. You've already done such a fantastic job that it will be one of the best weekends of my life. But I really wish you hadn't kept this from me. We're friends. We take the good with the bad. That's how it works.'

'You're right and how I ever thought I'd keep it from you for the whole weekend is anybody's business. I suppose I thought if I crossed my fingers and tried to keep a lid on it everything would be okay.'

Helen smiled. 'And how's that plan working out?'

Yaz's weak smile faded to nothing. 'You must have been mortified to see me go off like that. And in front of all your friends.'

'Don't even think about it. They'll all be fine with it. I promise.' She hesitated unsure whether to say more. 'Did you see it coming?'

Yaz began to cry. 'I had no idea,' she sobbed. 'It just came out of nowhere.'

Helen felt awful for making her relive the moment but now Yaz had confessed, the dam seemed to burst.

'I'd just finished putting the boys to bed when he came in and asked if he could have a quick word downstairs. I could see something wasn't right so we went into the kitchen and he just came out with it – he wasn't sure he wanted to be married any more – those were his exact words. It was horrible Helen, really horrible. And all the time he was talking I kept thinking to myself, "Please let me wake up and this just be a dream." '

Through her tears Yaz continued to pour her heart out. Simon had gone to live in the empty flat of one of his work colleagues who had just moved in with his girlfriend and had yet to get around to renting it out. They hadn't told the kids, so every morning he'd come over to help get them ready and every evening he'd come over to help tuck them into bed.

Helen was stunned. It didn't sound like the Simon

she knew. She wondered if Phil knew and had been keeping it a secret all this time. The thought made her stomach tighten and she squeezed her eyes shut until the sensation faded.

The very idea that Yaz and Simon had separated unsettled her greatly. While they were hardly anyone's idea of a perfect couple (Helen had lost count of the number of times she had watched Yaz mercilessly bully Simon in order to get her own way or observed Simon flip from normal to sullen over the smallest comment from Yaz) Helen had always felt that they worked. Somehow Yaz's volatility cancelled out Simon's own, leaving behind two reasonably decent people who loved each other a great deal even if they didn't always show it. To know that it was all at risk for something as intangible as one half of the unit needing 'space' upset her world view.

'So all of that stuff you said to me this morning . . . ?'

'Lies.'

Helen found it impossible to hide her surprise. Before this moment she would have described Yaz as the worst liar she had ever met.

'I know,' said Yaz as if reading her thoughts, 'it's funny how good you get at lying once you've run out of options.'

The buzz of conversation and laughter alerted the friends that they were no longer alone – lured by the beauty of the river a number of the hotel's guests were on their way down to the water's edge. Helen looked at Yaz and sighed.

'Do you want to go somewhere else?'

'No, I'm fine, really I am. Let's just try and get the evening back to where it was.'

The first sign that the evening might not be the washout Yaz had feared came as they arrived at the restaurant and spotted the girls sitting at a table for eight.

Delighted on Yaz's behalf, Helen quizzed the girls as to how this had come about.

'Yaz was right,' Kerry explained handing them each a glass of champagne. 'She had booked a table for eight. After you guys left Dee made a bit of a fuss and asked to speak to the manager and he double-checked the booking. Turns out the girl who took Yaz's call made a mistake and rather than amending the old booking she'd simply made a new one and made things worse by writing down Yaz's name as Mrs Cole so there was a whole table for eight sitting empty which was ours anyway. He was massively apologetic, promised to halve the bill for the evening and chucked in two bottles of Moët for our trouble!' Kerry raised her glass. 'I know we've gone a bit mad for the toasting tonight but who cares! Here's to Yaz, always right even when they try to tell her she's wrong!'

A Thai prawn noodle starter and mouthwatering steak main later, Helen was sitting in front of an empty coffee cup laughing as Lorna wheeled out the story of the time she and Dez had met David Bowie at Heathrow Airport and was so completely and utterly star-struck when he agreed to sign an autograph that she passed out, cracked her head on the floor and knocked herself unconscious. The girls loved Lorna's story, even those like Helen who had heard it before, and had it not been for Dee's suggestion that they all retire to the Silver Lounge for another drink, the conversation would no doubt have turned to other embarrassing celebrity encounters.

'Absolutely,' enthused Ros, 'I've been dying to sample some of those lovely cocktails you all had earlier.'

The other late arrivals, Heather and Carla, nodded in unison and en masse the girls went straight to the Silver Lounge where they commandeered a corner of the now bustling bar. The waiter distributed drinks menus, which they all studied – apart from Kerry, who seemed preoccupied.

'What's up?' asked Helen noticing her young friend's distraction.

'Look over there,' said Kerry pointing as subtly as she could to a tall, handsome man in a dark suit and tie who stood talking with a group of men who had their backs to her.

Helen was none the wiser. 'Who is he?'

Some of the other girls looked up to see what was monopolising their friends' attention.

'Is that who I think it is?' asked Lorna.

'Depends on who you think it is,' said Helen. 'I have no idea.'

'I don't know his name or anything,' said Kerry. 'But I'm pretty sure he's that Man United player. What's he doing here?'

'Same as us, probably,' said Helen. 'Having a weekend

away with his mates. Which means that the last thing he'll want is a group of women on a hen weekend gawping at him.'

Kerry wasn't convinced. 'Have you actually looked at him? He's absolutely beautiful.'

'And you're engaged!'

'And I wouldn't do anything! You know that but . . .' Kerry emitted what was intended to be a wistful sigh but which came out much closer to the low groan of a pervert. As one the entire table burst into peals of laughter.

Kerry was mortified. 'He heard you lot laughing and he looked over! I've got no chance with him now!'

Chuckling, Dee reached into her purse and slapped down ten pounds on the table. 'I'll give you a tenner if you talk to him.'

Lorna shook her head in mock dismay. 'Dee, don't be so cruel. Can't you see the girl's not up to it!'

'Kerry, ignore them, they're just jealous that you're still young and pretty not old and wizened like the rest of us!' defended Helen. 'Don't stoop to their level!'

Kerry contemplated the note on the table. 'What would I have to say?'

'Are you really going to do it?' screamed Dee in delight.

'I'll give you twenty pounds not to,' said Helen fearing the only way this escapade could end was badly.

'Like it's about the money!' chided Dee. 'She'd do it for free, that one!'

'You'll get us chucked out! And what if he's here with his girlfriend? She'll have your eyes out!'

'I'm only saying hello!' protested Kerry. 'There's no harm in that is there? I don't know . . . I was thinking maybe I might tell him that my Dan's a huge fan!'

Lorna cackled. 'Is that before or after you slip him your room number?'

Peering through her fingers Helen watched in horror as Kerry smoothed down her skirt and sashayed towards the footballer, her stomach tightening with her friend's every step. At the last moment Kerry lost her nerve and comically spun around one hundred and eighty degrees before the footballer had even noticed her.

Howling with laughter as Kerry returned to her seat, the girls all congratulated her bravery and even Dee declared that Kerry deserved the money.

Relieved that things hadn't got too out of hand, Helen called the waiter over to take their order and excused herself to use the loo, making sure to take the route furthest away from the footballer and his friends.

Emerging some moments later with freshly reapplied lipstick and hands that smelt of expensive moisturiser, Helen was about to head back to the bar when she was suddenly struck with the need to hear the voice of her fiancé. As anticipated, this thing with Simon and Yaz had disturbed her and she wanted Phil's reassurance that what had happened to their friends wouldn't happen to them too.

Helen searched her bag for her phone but then recalled her earlier decision to leave it in the bedroom in the spirit of freedom. She reckoned she had plenty of time to make a quick call and return to her friends before they sent out a search party and in a matter of minutes was breathlessly pushing her key card into her bedroom door.

Picking up her phone from the bedside table she called up Phil's number to the main screen and wondered if she was doing the right thing. He was supposed to be on a boys' weekend. What if he was annoyed that she was disturbing him or, even worse, think that she was checking up on him? She decided it would be okay as long as she told him why she had rung before he could say a word. If ever there was a justification for her call, the break-up of their friends' marriage fitted the bill. She pressed the call button and waited. There wasn't even a ringing tone. Instead, after a series of indeterminate clicks, she was directed to his voicemail.

Unsettled, she tried again but the same thing happened. Setting down the phone on the bed next to her she gave herself a good talking to as she began to worry. There were a million and one reasons why Phil's phone might have been switched off and none of them had any bearing on their relationship. He was no doubt in a pub or a club with the rest of the boys and had deliberately left his phone behind so he could concentrate on having a good time much like she had planned to do. She told herself she would see him soon enough anyway. She made one last attempt and this time she left a message: 'Hey you, it's just me saying a quick hello. Arrived safely, the hotel is amazing, and the girls are all here now and we're having a lot of fun. Obviously I'm not looking to cramp your style in front of the boys but I thought you might like to know that I love you madly! No need to ring me back, okay? Love you, bye.' Satisfied that she had done the right thing, she returned her phone to the bedside table and made her way downstairs to the lobby.

In the bar it was as though she had stepped into another world. The music that had previously been little more than aural wallpaper was now loud enough to be a feature in itself and that, combined with the buzz of a hundred different conversations, gave the room a whole different atmosphere.

Keen to avoid the footballer and his friends, Helen kept her head down as she passed where they had been standing and as she wove her way back to the girls Yaz looked up and waved. She raised her hand to wave back but felt a tap on her shoulder. She turned around to see a face, which – even though she hadn't encountered it in person for what felt like a lifetime – was instantly recognisable.

6.

In her professional life, Helen dealt exceptionally well with the unexpected. There was the time she was producing the breakfast show in Sheffield and the presenter, Jamie Toddington, fainted live on air in the middle of a phone interview with an MP who was trying to justify the closure of a local hospital. Before the MP had even become aware of the problem Helen had dropped her bowl of muesli, raced from her position at the control board to check that Jamie was still breathing, cued a traffic report and ran down to security requesting the assistance of someone with first aid training, while simultaneously placating the MP who was hanging on a second line wondering what was going on.

On another occasion working an afternoon shift during one of her early stints as a presenter, her producer had somehow failed to notice that the two main guests, a couple of former soap star heart-throb actors promoting a new production of *Waiting For Godot* at the local arts theatre, had turned up so drunk that they couldn't form a coherent sentence, unless it was to ask Helen if she had a boyfriend and to make crude sexual allusions. Helen had kicked both the actors out of her studio, called up the theatre press officer live on air to complain about their behaviour and then filled the remaining twenty-five minutes of the show getting listeners (a heady mix of retired ladies and mums gearing up for their second round of the school run) to nominate their top British actors most unlike the two reprobates who had contaminated her studio. As she passed over to the news desk and faded out her mic, she was besieged by co-workers congratulating her on a job well done.

In fact throughout her career both as producer and presenter she had not only managed to turn negatives into positives, but also to disguise the fact there'd even been a problem at all. That's how good Helen was at dealing with the unexpected. But professional Helen and private Helen were two very different creatures.

'You look like you might need to sit down.'

Helen stared at Aiden Reid, her former fiancé, the nation's most popular radio DJ and the only man to have broken her heart, with a look of utter disbelief. As is often the case with the least deserving, the intervening years had been kind to Aiden and though the ageing process had begun to take its toll around his eyes and around the temples, he was, Helen noted with some bitterness, even more handsome now than he had been when they were together.

Helen exhaled. She wanted this to be over. She wanted this to be over right now.

'My friends and I are just about to leave.'

Aiden grinned. 'And hello to you too. I'm sure you don't care what I think but you look great.'

'You're right,' said Helen pointedly, 'I don't care.'

'Don't be like that,' pleaded Aiden, 'I didn't come over to fight. I just wanted to say hello, that's all. I couldn't believe it when I saw you just now. Even though I could only see the back of you I knew straight away who it was. What are you doing here?'

'I'm here for a friend's hen weekend.'

Aiden laughed.

'What's so funny?'

'You'll never believe this but I'm actually here on a mate's stag weekend. What are the chances of that? The two of us here at the same time celebrating two different sets of impending nuptials.'

'Coincidences happen,' said Helen. 'It's not exactly what you'd call newsworthy, is it?'

'Maybe not,' replied Aiden. 'It's just that . . . I don't know . . . it's taken me by surprise seeing you here like this. And I'm guessing by the way you reacted that it took you a little by surprise too.'

Helen had no interest in confirming his suspicions. 'Who is it getting married?'

'Karl Peters.'

'The Five Live guy?'

Aiden nodded. 'Getting hitched to Ally Fallon. Really nice girl. She used to do a Saturday-morning kids' thing back in the day. Now she's mostly in radio.'

'I think I might have caught her show once but she

was so awful I had to switch her off. Karl though, I like him a lot, he's good. Very sharp, very strong, always on the ball.'

'And what about me?' Aiden stared at her keenly. 'I know it's not exactly your thing but you must have listened in at least once. If only out of curiosity.'

Helen shook her head even though this wasn't true. She had heard Aiden's Sony Award-winning show many times and although it verged on being self-indulgent rubbish at times, it was, for the most part, some of the best radio she had heard.

'You've never even listened once?'

'I hear the ratings are good though.'

'Through the roof.'

'You must be pleased.'

'More like ecstatic.' Grinning, he waved over Helen's shoulder.

'I take it those are the hens?'

Helen nodded and glanced over Aiden's shoulder at a group of men watching their every move. She recognised Karl Peters, the footballer that Kerry fancied, a couple of well-known TV actors and an Irish stand-up comedian. It was sickening; being famous was like belonging to an exclusive club where everybody knew each other.

'And I take it those are the stags?'

'Just a few of them. Do you want to come over and meet them? They don't bite.'

Helen could think of nothing she would rather do less. 'No, I'm good thanks. Like I said, we're supposed to be going soon so they're probably keen to make a move.'

'Yes, of course,' said Aiden. 'I mustn't keep you. It's been really good seeing you after all these years. You look . . . well, you look amazing. And I . . . I really do hope you have a great weekend.'

Although Helen wasn't a great believer in modern miracles, as she returned to the girls a small part of her naïvely hoped that her encounter with one of the country's biggest TV and radio stars might pass without comment. But within milliseconds of taking her seat her friends disabused her of this notion by collectively emitting an ear-piercing shriek of excitement.

'That's Aiden Reid you were just talking to!' shrieked Kerry. 'Aiden "off the radio!" Reid! I love him. He's just so funny and sparky. How do you know him, you dark horse? He's a bit of a ladies' man isn't he? Should a woman in your position be fraternising with such tabloid fodder?'

'I saw him in the paper the other day falling out of some private members' club in London with that young model that everyone's always going on about,' Dee chipped in, 'you know, the one who's always changing her hair colour?'

'Oh and let's not forget when he was half naked on the front cover of *Cosmo* last month,' added Ros. 'We had it up on the door of our office before HR made us take it down because they said it was creating an "inappropriate work environment".'

'I used to work with him,' said Helen. 'That's it. End of story.'

'End of story?' laughed Lorna, 'how can that be the end of the story when I'm only just finding out that sitting under my nose all this time has been the perfect person to introduce me to my future husband! He's gorgeous! We could have got hitched and had babies if you'd done the decent thing when I first met you and given me his phone number. What's he doing here?'

'He's with some friends for a stag do.'

'Who's the stag?'

'Karl Peters . . .'

'Karl Peters! That's the one!' interrupted Kerry. 'So who else is there? Any more famous types?'

'Listen,' said Yaz, exchanging glances with Helen, 'can't you leave the poor woman alone. She's just bumped into a bloke she used to work with who happens to be famous. Let's move on.'

'But we don't want to move on,' protested Lorna. 'Helen knows a celebrity! A genuine celebrity, not just someone who had a walk-on part in *Casualty*. We can't move on until we've had all the gory details. What's he really like?'

'He's fine,' said Helen charitably, 'we just don't get along that's all. Can we talk about something else?'

Lorna wouldn't let it go. 'What did he do to make you not like him? He always seems lovely on his show.'

'Put it this way,' said Helen, 'we didn't see eye to eye on certain issues and that, I'm afraid is all I have to say on the matter.'

The reason Helen's friends were unaware of her connection with Aiden Reid was simple: she had never told them. As Aiden's career had gone from strength to strength it had become clear to her that being the ex-fiancée of a celebrity was a burden in itself. She refused to allow herself to become just another paragraph in his biography and if keeping that part of her life secret from her friends as well as the tabloid press was the price to be paid in order to remain her own person then it was a price well worth paying.

In an effort to change the subject Yaz began telling the girls about the plans for the following morning but she had barely started when she was interrupted by one of the waiters.

'Excuse me, madam,' he began, 'Apologies for disturbing you, I hope you're all enjoying your evening. It's been brought to my attention that you're part of Mr Reid's party and as such the management of The Manor would like to invite you to be our guests for the rest of the evening in the Gold Lounge. If you'd like to follow me, I'll take you through.'

'You'd like to do what?' asked Helen.

'Invite you to the Gold Lounge, madam.'

'And that is what exactly?'

'A private function room that we reserve for special guests.'

The girls all looked at Helen in astonishment.

'He means celebrities!' gushed Kerry. 'He wants us to go to a special room with a bunch of celebrities!'

Helen felt an oncoming migraine hover overhead. 'Are you sure you've got the right table?'

'You are Ms Helen Richards aren't you?'

'I am,' said Helen nodding, 'but I'm definitely not part of Mr Reid's party and my friends and I are quite happy where we are, thank you very much.' She stood up to search for Aiden but the corner where he and his friends had been standing was empty.

'So, you would like me to inform Mr Reid that you won't be joining him?'

Helen felt a wave of indignation. Who did Aiden think he was that he could just snap his fingers and have her follow him about like that! She wasn't impressed by his money or his celebrity friends and she wanted him to know it. 'I'll tell you what I'd like,' spat Helen. 'I'd like you to tell Mr Reid that he can shove his special room right up his—' She stopped short and drew a deep calming breath like the ones she did in yoga class and held it until she felt less angry. 'Please, thank Mr Reid for his very kind offer but we're fine as we are.'

The waiter nodded and walked away, leaving Helen to face the questioning gaze of her friends. She downed what remained of her drink in a few long gulps. She wanted to go back to being happily drunk or retire to her room with a hot chocolate and one of the half dozen complimentary glossy magazines that resided there.

'Look,' she said finally, 'I know you all think it's mean but I really, really, really don't want to spend any time with him.'

'Of course,' said Kerry, 'but couldn't we just—?'

'No,' said Helen sharply. 'We can't *just* anything.'

Kerry looked equal parts embarrassed and annoyed. Helen immediately felt bad and apologised.

'It's fine,' said Kerry. 'You're right. He's probably not even half as nice as he is on the radio. They never are, are they?'

Helen felt even worse. She looked at the rest of the girls, who were all trying to avoid eye contact. If her ambition had been to kill the celebratory mood of the evening then she had quite clearly succeeded.

She looked to Yaz for advice. Yaz gave her a cheery wink, and addressed the girls. 'Look, radio star with celebrity friends or not it's not right that we let a bloke ruin our evening. We were having a cracking time before he turned up and I don't see why it shouldn't carry on. My suggestion is that we order a couple of bottles of wine and decamp to my room or Helen's and carry on the evening there.'

The girls began collecting their things together while Yaz called over the waiter to settle the bill. Helen stared into the middle distance feeling guilty. All her friends wanted was a bit of a laugh, something that they could tell their friends at work or the mums at the school gates about on Monday morning. With the possible exception of Ros, who had briefly worked for a women's magazine, their lives had never intersected with the world which Aiden inhabited. And while from her albeit limited knowledge she knew it to be a shallow, fickle world lacking in substance she also knew it was kind of fun too.

'Listen,' she said calling the girls to attention, 'I'm sorry. I've been a right whiney cow about all this and I've got no right to be. Give me a minute and I'll have you mixing with the great and the good before you know it.'

The delight on her friends' faces was enough to convince Helen that she had done the right thing. She went in search of the waiter, Yaz close at her heels. The horror on Yaz's face reassured her there was at least one person who understood what a big deal this was.

'What do you think he's up to?'

'I've no idea.'

'How was he when you spoke to him?'

'Fine. Chatty. Which was as well because I was too freaked out to say much of anything.'

'And you're sure you want to do this?'

'As long as you promise not to leave me alone with him.'

'Of course.'

'I mean it, Yaz, not for a second. I don't care if you're in mid-conversation with one of his footballer mates or the head of the BBC, do not leave me alone with him.'

'I promise, he won't get anywhere near you.'

'And I don't want him knowing why we're here, either.'

'Fine.'

'And I don't want any of the girls talking about me to him or any of his friends. Not where I live, not what I'm doing, who I'm with or even what I had for dinner tonight.'

Yaz gave Helen's hand a reassuring squeeze. 'Maybe we shouldn't be doing this if you still feel this way. I was just thinking we'd drink his champagne, flirt with his mates and have a bit of a laugh but the last thing I want is for you to get upset.'

'I'll be fine,' replied Helen, 'Promise. Drinking his champagne, flirting with his mates and having a laugh sounds perfect. That's the least he can do after everything he put me through.'

Helen found the waiter and informed him that she had changed her mind.

'This is going to be amazing,' said Carla on Helen's return. 'What am I going to say if they ask me what I do for a living? I can't tell them I'm a social worker!'

Lorna chuckled. 'Tell them you're a glamour model, that's what I'm going to do if I get anywhere near that Aiden fella!' She hoisted her ample bosom in comedic fashion to the delight of her friends.

The waiter led them towards the rear of the bar, where there was a gold painted door where a female member of staff dressed in the hotel's grey uniform stood holding a clipboard. The waiter gave her a discreet nod and she stepped aside.

Helen ushered the rest of the girls through the doorway but at the last moment tapped Yaz on the shoulder.

'I can't do this,' said Helen.

'I thought you were fine,' replied Yaz.

'So did I but . . . but . . .'

'But what?'

'I've just got a bad feeling about it. Like . . . I don't know . . . I just don't want to be in the same room as him.'

'Then I won't go either,' replied Yaz. 'We'll nip back to my room and get drunk on the mini-bar.'

'You have to,' said Helen. 'The girls will need keeping an eye on. Just tell them I had a headache or something. They'll be having too good a time to care.'

'And what will you do?'

'Have an early night,' said Helen. 'But don't think for a minute that I won't want to hear every last juicy detail in the morning.'

Saturday

7.

Helen had never been a huge fan of the Saturday-morning lie-in. Most weekends she was out of bed, throwing on her gym kit and halfway out of the door to the local fitness centre by half past seven at the latest. Any longer lying in bed and she would have felt like she was stewing in her own filth just for the sake of it. So it was something of a surprise when she opened her eyes that Saturday morning, fumbled blindly in the darkness of her room for her phone and discovered from its digital display that not only had she managed to sleep past her usual wake-up time but was even in danger of missing the prearranged nine o'clock breakfast rendezvous with the rest of the girls, which was bound to go down about as well as her early disappearance the night before.

Helen was not sure what to make of the evening's events. It all felt like some elaborate dream from which she had been unable to wake herself. First the bombshell about Simon and Yaz separating, then bumping into Aiden, it was almost as if her subconscious mind was doing everything it could to unsettle her as she prepared to be married. The only problem was her subconscious had nothing to do with it. This was reality, bad luck, and even worse timing.

No one was more surprised by the strength of her reaction to Aiden than Helen herself. It had been such a long time since they had been together that she had long since ceased to consider the man on the pages of the *Sun*'s Bizarre column as anything other than a stranger and the idea that they had once been very much in love seemed unreal.

Still, there was no doubting the emotional veracity of her reaction towards him. This man, this stranger, whom she had succeeded in telling herself she could barely even recall, had turned her world upside down. First, by re-entering her life and second, by exposing her to an unwelcome truth: after all these years he still had the power to upset her.

It wasn't fair. Aiden meant nothing to her, she was sure. How many times as she skimmed the daily newspapers for her show had she come across reports of Aiden in the tabloids and not felt a thing? How many times had she heard his disembodied voice promoting some new car insurance product or cat food on TV and dismissed his rude interjection into her life without a second thought? He meant nothing to her. Absolutely nothing. And yet seeing him in the flesh at the same hotel changed everything. No longer an easily dismissed abstraction from the past, he instead became a living, breathing reminder of one of the unhappiest periods of her life, a time when she had been prepared to hold back nothing from someone whom she believed she could trust completely and who had thrown it all – the love, the trust, the devotion – back in her face.

At the time Helen had wanted revenge, for Aiden to endure first-hand the torment that she had lived through as she cried herself to sleep night after night. But as time progressed and her desire to heal overcame her craving for justice, she finally reached the point where she knew the only way for her to move forward was to let go of the past – and that included all feelings of hatred towards Aiden. So she let go. Or at least she thought she had.

But did her reaction to Aiden the night before mean that she hadn't quite left him behind? Did the surge of anger and the flood of adrenalin she had felt as she beheld the face that she had once loved mean that she had been in denial all this time? She thought about Phil's: *You know as well as I do that this is all about him. It always has been and it always will be.* Had Phil been able to see the truth when she had been blind? The idea made her shudder. Whatever the answers to these many questions, she needed to stay away from Aiden and talk to Phil as soon as possible.

She dialled Phil's number and again the call went straight through to his voicemail. She opened her mouth to leave a message but the words wouldn't come and after a number of moments listening to the silence that she was supposed to be filling she ended the call.

He was fine, she reassured herself. The most likely scenario was that his battery was dead and he had forgotten his charger. Half convinced by her reasoning she tried to recall if Phil had told her the name of the hotel they were staying at but nothing sprang to mind. She'd asked several times and he'd replied that it was 'all in hand' – whatever that meant. She wondered if Simon had told Yaz where he'd be, but given her friend's recent news she could never ask the question.

She told herself to remain calm and turned on the bedside light. She was immediately cheered by the sight of the illuminated room as its luxury reminded her that she was supposed to be having a good time. With this in mind she climbed out of bed, made her way to the bathroom and turned on the shower. The rainfall showerhead burst into life forcing out sizzling jets of steaming water on to the zinc floor beneath. Helen shed her pyjamas, laid them on the ornate bench at the side of the shower and strode into the revitalising waterfall. Some fifteen minutes later, having been pummelled by the pounding water, Helen re-emerged feeling like she was ready to take on the day ahead.

With her hair done, make-up on and having spent longer than was strictly necessary working out what to wear to breakfast, Helen had tidied her room so as not to totally disgust the chambermaid when there was a sharp knock at the door. She cursed herself for not having woken up earlier, dashed into the bathroom to pick up yesterday's knickers from the floor, tossed them under the duvet and opened the door.

'Yaz,' she said breathing a huge sigh of relief. 'Come in.'

'Who were you expecting?'

'Long story.' Helen fished out her underwear from beneath the duvet and tucked it into the bottom of her case. 'I just wish I'd got up earlier that's all. Sleep well?'

'For what felt like the ten minutes I was there, yes.'

Yaz sat down on the edge of the bed, cupping her head in her hands, while Helen opened a bottle of water, poured some into a glass and handed it to her friend.

'I take it that it was a bit of a rough one then?'

' "Rough" would have been a welcome mercy,' said Yaz. 'I have nothing but admiration for your decision to go to bed early last night. Honestly, if it wasn't for the fact I'm looking forward to a day of pure, unadulterated relaxation rather than sitting at home screaming at the kids to stop killing each other I'd be feeling pretty sorry for myself.'

'But you had fun?'

Yaz nodded wearily and between sips of water said: 'Best. Time. Ever.'

'So what happened then?'

'Obviously the girls were really sorry that you didn't come but I think they all sensed why and for a little while we all felt out of our depth. But then Aiden came over and introduced himself and his friends and from then we didn't look back. Honestly, it was like a walk through the pages of *Heat* magazine. The girls and I would be talking to one famous guy and another would appear out of nowhere and offer to top up my champagne glass.'

Helen winced. The thought of her friends being plied with alcohol by a group of Aiden's friends on the first night of their stag weekend made her feel queasy. 'They were on their best behaviour, weren't they?'

Yaz cackled and Helen felt glad to have her old friend back. 'Sadly they were all absolute gents. Even that Irish comedian fella – who we all had down as a bit of a letch. In fact all he did was show us pictures of his kids on his phone. It was a great night though, Helen, you should have come. All we did was laugh, knock back champagne and listen to their absolutely outrageous stories about other celebrities.'

'And Aiden?' Helen hated herself for asking the question but she knew it had to be done.

'Do you really want to know?'

'No, you're right,' said Helen quickly. 'I don't.'

Yaz tried to read her friend's mind. 'He was fine,' she said. 'He did ask after you, and I don't think he was taken in by your headache story but I can't fault him as a host. He looked after us well, kept us entertained and didn't ask about you at all.'

'Nothing?'

Yaz shook her head. 'Only why you weren't there.'

'Good,' said Helen even though she was sure it didn't all add up. 'Then let's go and get some breakfast. I'm starving.'

Helen could barely keep a straight face as she

and Yaz entered the restaurant and spotted the girls at the rear of the room looking like they were at death's door.

'You know I love you lot dearly,' said Helen as she sat down at the table, 'and it pains me to tell you this, but you look terrible!'

'Just sit down and stop bellowing, Richards,' wailed Lorna, who had been resting her head on her folded arms. 'Some of us are hurting inside.'

Helen squeezed into the banquette seating next to Lorna and Dee and then stroked Lorna's head mockingly. 'Awwww, did someone have a few too many shandies last night?'

Lorna groaned and pushed Helen's hand away. 'This is your revenge isn't it for that time I made you go clubbing last summer.'

'Oh, yes, indeed,' grinned Helen, 'you're the reason I haven't been able to go anywhere near a vodka gimlet for the last year without immediately feeing nauseous. How does it feel now, my friend?'

'You do know that I hate you, don't you?'

'Well if I didn't,' said Helen kissing the top of her friend's head, 'I certainly do now.'

Breakfast for the majority was brief as might be expected with such a high concentration of hangovers, and mainly consisted of black coffee, roughly three quarters of the fresh fruit that had been laid out on the buffet and wholemeal toast all round. But despite the low moans alternating with various pledges to never touch the demon drink again, Helen could see that her friends were secretly rather pleased that they still had what it took to party like nineteen-year-olds.

The girls' account of the night before pretty much mirrored Yaz's. Aiden had been sweet, his celebrity friends entertaining and the evening so far removed from their everyday lives as to make it an anecdote they would be dining out on for a long while. None of them, even in passing, mentioned Aiden asking questions about Helen.

'Are you sure?' asked Helen as she and Kerry picked at a bowl of blueberries. 'Not a single question about me?'

Kerry raised an eyebrow. 'You sound almost disappointed. Are you sure there was never anything between you? I can easily imagine you being his type.'

'And what's that supposed to mean?'

'You know. Beautiful and feisty. Those girls that he's always falling out of nightclubs with, they'd be no challenge. But someone like you, someone he'd have to work hard to impress, oh, you'd be right up his street.'

Helen laughed. 'I think someone's watched one too many Sandra Bullock movies!'

'So why the interest in what he talked about last night?'

'Because.'

'Is that all I'm getting? Now you're really starting to worry me. You don't fancy him do you?'

'No, of course not.'

'Then what?'

'Look,' sighed Helen. 'Back when I knew him he did some pretty awful things to a friend of mine that I find it hard to forgive him for. If he's being nice to me, it's only because he's trying to get to her, the person he knew all that time ago, and well, I know for a fact that she's not interested so I'd prefer it if we all keep him at arm's length. Is that okay?'

Kerry nodded. 'Of course. I had no idea he was like that. He seems like such a nice bloke.'

'They always do,' said Helen, 'in the beginning at least.'

Helen plucked another blueberry from the bowl, coating her teeth with its sweet, gooey flesh, while much to her relief Kerry was drawn into a discussion Dee was having with Lorna about the best place to buy MAC make-up in Nottingham. Helen wished that she had never brought up the subject of Aiden; it was telling how in the space of a few moments she had already amplified Kelly's innocent comment far beyond its worth. The madness from which she was trying to protect herself was already leaking out into the real world and if she wasn't careful more would follow.

Yaz stood up and called for everyone's attention. 'You should have received emails confirming what treatments you're booked in for during the weekend and when but I've got copies for anyone who hasn't brought theirs along. The first session is a group mani-pedi at eleven on the dot but for those who need a detox beforehand – naming no names – some of us are heading to the steam room in ten minutes so if you do want to come along grab your things, and we'll all head down to the spa together.'

Relieved to have someone taking charge the girls

began making their way back to their rooms, slowing down only to congratulate Yaz on being so organised and to tell Helen what a good time they were having.

'How right they are,' said Helen as the last of her friends disappeared. 'This weekend is amazing. I honestly don't think anything could—'

'What is it?' asked Yaz as Helen stopped abruptly. 'It's not lover boy and his mates again is it?'

'No,' sighed Helen as every iota of positive energy she possessed drained from her. 'You know how it is when you're having such a great time that you totally forget about the fact that you invited your scheming bitch-faced sister-in-law on your hen weekend until the moment she arrives? Well that's what.'

8.

There were very few people whom Helen actively disliked. In fact if she had to name them individually (with the exception of Aiden Reid) only three people would spring to mind. The first was Chantelle Roberts who made the list because from the day Helen met her at Edgehill infant school until the day she left to go to a nearby private school Chantelle made it her mission to make Helen's life a living hell with a subtle but none the less destructive cycle of constant befriending and defriending. On any given day the six-year-old Helen would turn up to school expecting to spend her break time playing 'In the witch's den', only to discover that for some reason known only to Chantelle, Helen had fallen out of favour and would have to spend break walking around the playground looking up at the sky so that no one could see she was crying.

The second person on her list was Morwenna Kavell, who was Helen's boss for six months when she worked at Cardiff FM. Helen never knew exactly what it was that this woman hadn't liked about her (although she speculated about it frequently) but it seemed to be more than enough to turn someone who on the surface seemed both reasonable and professional, into a scheming psycho who devoted every waking moment during the time that they worked together to finding new and inventive ways of making Helen's life unbearable.

The third and final person was the regional sales director of a Milton Keynes based communications solutions firm, a mistress in the ancient art of one-up-manship and a total cow who happened to be related to the man Helen loved. Worse, she was currently making her way across the restaurant towards them.

'Caitlin,' said Helen kissing her sister-in-law-to-be on the cheek. She stood back to take in Caitlin's immaculately groomed form and felt instantly depressed. 'How are you? How was the journey?'

'An absolute nightmare. Best part of an hour sitting on the M1 just past Leicester. Nearly gave up and turned back! It would've been a shame of course, after all this place isn't cheap, but as it happens I'm off to a new country spa hotel just outside Buckinghamshire in a few weeks that by all reports should knock the spots off this place. Still, here I am, always doing the right thing!'

'Well I'm glad you did,' lied Helen, resisting the temptation to throttle Caitlin. 'The weekend wouldn't have been the same without you.'

Caitlin flashed her best professional smile, the one Helen felt sure she used whenever closing a business deal. 'You say the sweetest things.' She held out her hand to Yaz and although she couldn't be sure Helen thought she detected an extra glint of spitefulness in Caitlin's eye. 'And Yaz, how are you? Long time no see.'

'Yes,' said Yaz. 'It has been a long time. Been keeping well?'

'Can't complain,' replied Caitlin, carefully. 'You? How are those adorable kids of yours? Still running you ragged? I don't know how you do it. I can't see me ever having kids. They're a guaranteed route to a ruined figure.'

Yaz's face fell as it dawned on her that she had just been Caitlined. Helen was confused; normally Caitlin saved her catty remarks for Helen alone but for some reason she appeared to want to drag Yaz into this too. Realising she had milliseconds to stop Yaz slapping her sister-in-law-to-be into next week Helen quickly jumped into the fray and changed the subject.

'We're all going down to the sauna in a minute,' she said quickly. 'If you hurry up and get changed you can join us.'

Caitlin raised a eyebrow. 'It always takes me forever to unpack so I doubt I'll make it. Otherwise what time should I meet you for the first treatment?'

'Eleven o'clock, in the spa.'

'Great,' said Caitlin. She flashed Helen and Yaz another of her business smiles and then with one swish of her ponytail she clip-clopped out of the restaurant leaving the speechless friends wondering what had just hit them.

'I always knew she was a bitch,' said Yaz, 'but that woman takes bitchdom to a whole new level! She's like a super-turbo-charged-bitch-faced bitch.'

Helen nodded in agreement. 'And . . . might I add, a right royal pain in the arse too.'

'You have my deepest sympathies becoming family with a woman like that. My deepest sympathies indeed.'

In the beginning Helen had rationalised Caitlin's dislike as simple loyalty to her close friend Beth, whom Phil had dated for two years. Caitlin regularly hung out with Phil and Beth and so when Phil called time on the relationship it spelled not only the end of the couple but also for Caitlin spending time with her brother whom she idolised. Seemingly convinced that Phil and Beth were in the throes of getting back together, Caitlin had extended a somewhat frosty reception when Phil had invited her to meet Helen for the first time. Phil had picked up on his sister's hostility but had excused it in that lazy way all men excuse the behaviour of women they like: 'She's not being bitchy,' he explained, 'she just doesn't know you that's all. Give her time and she'll soon warm up.'

The second time was some six months later when Phil decided it was time to introduce Helen to his mum and stepdad and so organised a Sunday afternoon barbecue for his entire family. Helen had hoped that relations between them would improve over time but in fact they became worse. While never openly hostile, Caitlin focused on one-upping Helen whenever the opportunity arose. If Helen told a story about a great weekend, Caitlin would tell a story about an even better one. If Helen bought a new dress and wore it out to dinner, Caitlin made sure to let everyone know how new her own dress was and how expensive it had been. Whatever Helen did that was good, Caitlin had always done better. And because it wasn't open hostility Phil didn't see it. 'Honestly babe,' he told her as they cleared away after the barbecue when after much deliberation she had finally brought the subject up, 'you're just being paranoid. So what if she's a bit boastful? If she winds you up that much just ignore her.'

Helen tried to take Phil's advice and although months went by without the two of them needing to exchange a word, what with Christmas, Easter and various family birthdays there were other times when there was literally no escaping Caitlin. And although it would be natural to assume that over nine years, two family bereavements, and the handing over of countless tastefully selected and perfectly wrapped birthday and Christmas presents (presents that had quite clearly not been bought or wrapped by Phil), that hostilities would have ceased, this was not the case. Instead they continued to bubble under the surface waiting for the opportunity to erupt.

Inviting Caitlin to the hen weekend was Helen's final olive branch to Caitlin for the sake of the man she loved and if she refused to accept it after this weekend, or at the latest after the wedding, she resolved to stop making the effort and cut Caitlin out of her life for good.

Helen was up in her room frantically stuffing one of the hotel's tastefully designed straw tote bags with everything she needed for the morning when her phone rang.

'It's me,' said Yaz urgently. 'Listen I don't want to panic you, but we might not have thought this whole thing with Caitlin through properly.'

Helen hadn't got a clue what Yaz was talking about.

'Think about it. We've just invited her to meet downstairs in the lobby haven't we? Now I know she said she probably won't come but what if she does and gets there before we do, introduces herself and the girls start telling her about what an amazing time they all had hanging out with Aiden? I don't know whether you'd planned to tell Phil about bumping into your ex or not but if she gets to the girls before we do I guarantee you won't need to worry about how to break the news to him.'

Yaz was right. This was exactly the kind of thing Caitlin would leap on. Grabbing her bag, Helen snatched up her key card and ran out of the room slamming the door behind her. Racing along the corridor at top speed she passed the lift and took the stairs, then pelted down several steps at a time.

Her heart pounding as if it was trying to escape her chest, Helen sprinted to reception to meet the girls.

'I need to tell you something,' gasped Helen thankful that there was no sign of Caitlin. 'Is everyone here?'

'All except Yaz,' said Kerry.

'Look,' said Helen quickly, 'it's like this: for reasons that I don't want to go into I need to ask you all a massive favour. Whatever you do don't—'

Helen stopped abruptly as Yaz arrived frantically waving her hands.

'What?'

'Nothing,' said Yaz still waving her arms. 'I'm just thinking that you probably need to stop talking . . . now.'

Realising something was up Helen was horrified to see Caitlin standing behind her. In that instant Helen saw she had two options: she could allow herself to fall apart as she had done when she bumped into Aiden or professional Helen could get on with the business of being unflappable.

'Caitlin,' said Helen calmly, 'great you've decided to join us. I was just getting the girls together to explain that they shouldn't . . . drink too much.'

Caitlin looked confused. 'Isn't that sort of the idea of hen weekends?'

Clearly in agreement the others looked on perplexed.

'I'm just saying that—' An idea occurred to her and she pointed to Caitlin. 'Where are my manners? Everybody, this is Phil's sister, Caitlin, everybody this is Caitlin.'

It wasn't exactly the most subtle of ways of getting her point across to her friends that they should keep their mouths shut about the events of the night before, but from the raised eyebrows and silent gasps that spread amongst the girls like a Mexican wave the message had clearly been received. But just to make sure that there weren't any little slip-ups as everyone introduced themselves to Caitlin,

Helen whispered to Yaz to brief everyone individually about what was and what wasn't out of bounds to talk about with the evil one.

The girls made their way out of reception and along the outside path to the Spa. It was a beautiful cloudless morning, the perfect summer barbecue day and even though it was only mid-morning there was no doubt it was going to be a scorcher.

The area around the spa had been landscaped so that it was only once visitors descended the limestone stairs that the spa could be seen at all. Once there the girls knew they were in for a treat. The front entrance looked like a partially buried glass dome jutting out of the slope and as the girls marvelled at its architectural elegance the more confident they became that a building like this wasn't going to be staffed by bored teens fresh out of beauty school.

Signing in, they made their way to the changing rooms where they hurriedly undressed and within a matter of minutes they were settled in the steam room and getting down to the main business of the day: conversation.

'So Helen,' began Ros, 'How are all the wedding plans going? I bet you had it all sewn up months ago. You've always been the most organised person I know.'

'Oh, you know how it is,' said Helen, quickly. She wiped her sweat-laden brow with her towel. 'Even when you're organised, with something this big there are always things to do.'

As those who had experience began to exchange tales of their own wedding organisational nightmares, Helen reflected on Ros's comment. It was true that she was highly organised; there was no way she could do her current job as a presenter and have fulfilled her role as a producer successfully without being organised, and yet she had somehow neglected to bring that same degree of organisational control to bear on what was supposed to be one of the most important days of her life. It wasn't just that she had left the booking of the venue, the hiring of the caterers and the sorting out of the honeymoon to Phil (she argued that as he was his own boss he had more free time to do these things), it was that with less than a week to go she still hadn't decided on a dress.

Since the first of her university friends began to get married Helen had had an image in her head of the perfect wedding dress so when Aiden had proposed, she set to work on making the dream become a reality by gathering together pictures ripped from magazines along with brief sketches of her own. Once she was satisfied that she had all the inspiration she needed she went to see the woman who had designed Yaz's cousin's gown which she had admired some months before.

The designer had seemed to understand what Helen wanted straight away and had shown her some beautiful swatches of material, which Helen knew would be perfect. Several fittings later and there it was: the fantasy dress of her dreams, a more beautiful reality than she'd ever expected: a floor length strapless ivory satin sheath dress exquisitely embroidered with antique beads and trimmed with vintage ribbon.

Gazing at her reflection in the mirror at the final fitting Helen felt every inch the princess that she had hoped to be. She had left the dressmaker's nearly a thousand pounds poorer but with a joy in her heart she would have gladly paid ten times more to possess.

When she called off the wedding, the dress was the one aspect of the cancelled day that she wouldn't allow anyone else to deal with, torn as she was between keeping it and giving it away. In the end, having bagged it up and driven to the other side of the city with the intention of donating it to a charity shop, she just couldn't do it. As selfish as it was she couldn't bear the thought of another woman walking down the aisle in her dream dress and she took the bag from the boot of the car, crossed over to the car park of a nearby pub and with tears streaming down her face threw the dress into an industrial waste container and walked away.

'Are you having any, Helen?'

Helen stared blankly at Heather. She hadn't got a clue what was being asked of her.

'You're a million miles away,' teased Heather. 'It must be all this steam! I was just asking are you having wedding favours on the table? I went to a wedding last summer and the couple were real green freaks and had put several packets of seeds on every table for people to take away and plant so as to offset the carbon footprint of the wedding!'

Helen was panic-stricken. 'I hadn't even thought about it.'

Heather looked mortified. 'Sorry, babe! I didn't mean to wind you up into a frenzy. It must be the full-time mum in me: I don't feel normal unless I'm armed with a sixteen-page to-do list! Just step out of this circle of madness, I say, and do your own thing!'

Helen smiled weakly. Party favours were the least of her problems. At this rate she would be getting married in a tracksuit and slippers. She and Yaz had been looking at dresses for months now, starting with a wedding fair at the NEC in Birmingham and branching out to every bridal shop within a thirty-mile radius of Nottingham. And while there had been many hideous creations amongst the dresses she had seen (one in particular, a huge hideous pink meringue that could easily have been the star of its own TV documentary entitled *My biggest gypsy wedding*), there had also been plenty of tasteful and elegant dresses with which she had fallen in love. A cream taffeta dress in a bridal shop in Hucknall and another that could have been plucked straight from the set of a sumptuous Merchant Ivory production to name but two. And yet whenever the shop assistant asked if she would like to come back for a second fitting her response was always: 'I do really like it but I'm going to carry on looking just that little while longer.' And to anyone who asked what her dress was like (a question aimed at her on an almost daily basis) her reply was the same: 'Beautiful. But I'm not saying anything as I don't want to spoil the surprise.'

Helen knew it was madness to leave it this late and that even if she were to walk into a wedding dress shop first thing on Monday morning and choose the first dress, no matter how hideous, that she laid eyes on there was every chance that – this being July – they would be so overwhelmed with orders that even if she offered to pay them double they might not be able to get any alterations done by the Saturday morning. And what kind of bride doesn't have a dress a week before her wedding day?

9.

It was approaching midday and the first beauty treatment of the day was complete. The girls stood in a circle in the changing rooms admiring the results of their joint manicure and pedicure.

'What's yours called again?' asked Yaz, looking down at Helen's feet.

'Boutique Trash,' said Helen.

'So that's pink then,' said Yaz.

'Looks like it,' said Helen. She looked over at Lorna's toes. 'I like yours Lorna. What's that one?'

'Burnt Sunrise,' said Lorna.

'So that's dark orange then,' said Yaz.

'I hate my feet,' said Dee.

They all inspected Dee's feet. 'Don't say that,' said Helen. 'You've got great feet.'

'No,' said Dee. 'My ex used to say I'd got Hobbit feet and he had a point. Just call me Bilbo Baggins.'

'I know you were married to him and everything,' said Helen, 'but your ex was more than a bit of an idiot. Your feet are beautiful and don't let anyone tell you otherwise.'

'I wish I had feet like Caitlin's,' said Dee, 'Just look at them. They're perfect.'

Everyone looked at Caitlin's feet. Much as Helen loathed her, even she had to agree that in the world of feet Caitlin's were right up there with those of Natalie Portman, Jennifer Anniston and Halle Berry.

'She's right,' chipped in Ros, 'They are gorgeous. That colour really suits you too.'

'Thank you girls,' said Caitlin beaming, 'it's weird but whenever I'm out in my strappy sandals I get loads of compliments about them.'

Helen smiled inwardly at the thought of people queuing in nightclubs just to get a glimpse of her sister-in-law-to-be's feet.

'I think we've all got great feet,' said Helen diplomatically, in a bid to move the conversation on. 'And we should definitely give them an airing when we go out tonight. Who's up for it?' Helen counted up the hands. The vote was unanimous.

'Toes out for the lads it is!' laughed Carla who had been single so long that she feared it might become permanent. 'I've got a good feeling that Gunmetal Rose is going to be my lucky colour!'

Fully dressed, the girls made their way out of the spa with the conversation focused evenly between what they fancied for lunch and how long they would need to get ready to go out to dinner that evening. Helen herself was happy that for a few moments at least she wasn't thinking about wedding dresses and was content to listen to the others but as they headed to the restaurant her heart stopped. Aiden and two of his friends were coming towards them.

From her position at the back of the group Helen could see from the body language of her friends that they were unsure how to react. Most of them simply chose to ignore Aiden and his friends while others, never having had to blank a complete stranger with whom they had spent half the night drinking, offered an embarrassed half wave that Helen hoped had gone unseen by Caitlin.

But Aiden had seen Helen and fully intended to try and talk to her.

'What are you going to do?' asked Yaz, quickly. 'Do you want me to go over and tell him you can't speak?'

Helen shook her head. 'No, you carry on to the restaurant. Tell the girls I'll be along in a minute but don't wait and whatever you do don't let Caitlin out of your sight.'

Helen's breathing deepened involuntarily as she began to walk towards Aiden who was standing in the middle of the grass. She wondered whether he was going to make her walk all the way over to him but then he began to walk towards her.

'Morning,' said Aiden as they met halfway.

'Morning.'

'Just been to the spa?'

Helen nodded. 'We all had our nails done.' She dangled her newly manicured hands in the air as if he needed proof.

'Nice,' he replied studying them. 'You won't believe this but I had manicures for a while. Back in the early days I was doing a cable show, my agent clocked how filthy my nails were and so she set up regular appointments for the eight weeks I was doing the show and then billed the cable company.'

'And did you enjoy them?'

Aiden shrugged. 'Not enough to carry on. It's too much of a detail thing. Us blokes are too big-picture orientated to think whizzing into town to have some bird do our nails and make small talk is worth the effort.'

Helen laughed. 'It's hard to know what to do first: marvel at the ease with which you can insult half the population with your simplistic worldview or ask a follow up question about what this so-called "big-picture" is that you'd rather be doing than appear on TV looking like you spend your spare time rooting through rubbish bins.'

'What can I say?' asked Aiden. 'I'm a guy. We don't sweat the small stuff.' He shifted his weight uneasily. Helen could feel a question coming.

'Did your friends enjoy last night?'

'Yes, thanks. Obviously some of them were a little worse for wear this morning, but they were pretty unanimous about having had a good time. Thanks for that, it was really good of you.'

'It was nothing. They're a great bunch of girls and the lads really enjoyed being around them but I can't say that you weren't missed.'

Helen blushed. 'Thank you. And I apologise. It's just that it had been an incredibly long day and I was shattered. I guarantee you, I'd have been no fun at all.'

Aiden nodded as though he understood but Helen

didn't think for a moment that he believed a single word she had said.

'I know this is awkward for you,' he began, 'and well . . . it's awkward for me too. But isn't it weird that of all the places we could be this weekend we're both here? Maybe this is a good opportunity for us to clear the air.'

'You're not trying to tell me that you, world renowned sceptic Aiden Reid, believe in something as airy-fairy as fate? Next thing you'll be telling me that you Cosmic Ordered this whole thing up.'

Aiden laughed. 'Look, all I'm saying is that we're here and the chances of that were pretty slim. So why not make the most of it?'

'And do what?'

'Give me half an hour of your time.'

Helen sighed. Had she walked a bit faster she could have avoided this whole sorry saga. 'Fine,' she said. 'But make it ten minutes.'

Aiden began walking purposefully though it soon became apparent that he wasn't sure where he was going.

'What exactly are you looking for?' asked Helen as they reached the far edge of the hotel.

'I'll know it when I see it.'

'Some things never change.'

'What's that supposed to mean?'

'I'm just thinking about the summer you were supposed to be best man for your friend Mike's wedding in Darlington. Only we didn't get there until—'

'—the whole thing was over!'

'And all because you absolutely refused to ask for directions to the church.'

Aiden chuckled. 'Mike was so annoyed about having to get his granddad to do the honours that he didn't speak to me for months. I can't believe you're still going on about that.'

'What can I say?' replied Helen. 'Some things are too amusing to forget.'

They continued down a tree-lined path that eventually reached a slow running stream. There were a number of smart-looking modern loungers and wooden benches scattered around under the trees but it was quiet and empty.

'I read about this spot in the brochure,' said Helen. 'I'd planned to come down here at some point and read my book.'

'See,' said Aiden. 'And there was you thinking I didn't know where I was going. That's the genius of me: appearing haphazard but actually in total control.'

Helen didn't comment, knowing full well that any attempt at a retort would only stoke his ego further. It was lovely though. Peaceful. Serene. It made her feel disconnected from the rest of the world. Like she was stepping out of place and time.

'So how's Karl getting on? Are you making sure he's having a good weekend?'

'It's hard to tell. We could have bought him a Ferrari and had a naked Scarlett Johansson pop out of a cake to hand him the keys and I swear if it happened the week before the new RAJARs were due out he still wouldn't raise a smile. He's one of life's worriers.'

'Not like you. You've *never* worried about audience figures.'

'That was the old me,' said Aiden picking up on Helen's sarcasm. 'The new me is a nervous wreck. Anyway, how are the ratings for your show?'

'Pretty solid.'

'Now that you can listen to local radio on the internet I do catch your show from time to time. It's good stuff.'

'Thanks, but it's hardly the groundbreaking arena of rock 'n' roll breakfast is it?'

'Which is why it's harder. I couldn't do afternoons to save my life. In the morning everything's fresh. I'm breaking news stories and waking up the audience to a brand new day. By the time your show starts the new has become the old and the audience are already thinking about what they've got to do tomorrow, there's literally nothing to work with. That's why you're doing such a great job making a solid show against the odds. I swear if they put you on breakfast you'd slay me.'

Helen sat down on the nearest bench and looked at the stream where a group of ducks were congregating amongst the reeds. Aiden sat down next to her.

'I'm getting married next weekend,' said Helen.

Aiden was silent. A sparrow landed on the branch of a silver birch and after a moment checking its surroundings flew to the headrest of one of the sun loungers and surveyed them keenly.

'I thought you said—'

'I lied,' she said quickly.

'Because?'

'Because you don't have any right to know about me.'

Aiden nodded. The sparrow flew to the ground a few yards away from their feet, pecked at a clump of moss and then with what looked like some kind of beetle in its beak flew back to the silver birch.

'Is he a good man? I know that's kind of a stupid question given that you're marrying him, but you know what I mean. Is he everything you're looking for?'

Helen shook her head. 'I'm not going to do this.'

'Do what?'

'Take part in whatever's going on in your head.'

'Then why are you here?'

Helen stood up and began walking back up the path towards the hotel.

'Listen,' called Aiden. 'Stop. I'm sorry, okay? I was bang out of order.' Helen continued to the top of the hill from where she could see the hotel. She heard Aiden running up the path behind her. 'Look, stop,' he said as he finally caught up with her. 'Don't let's leave things like this. I'm sorry, okay? It was a stupid thing to say. Your news just took me by surprise that's all.'

'And why should that be?' asked Helen. 'It was no big surprise to me when you got married.'

'And look how that ended.'

'Do you want me to feel sorry for you?'

'No,' said Aiden, 'but I do want you to know that you're the reason it didn't work.'

Before Helen could muster a response she spotted Caitlin walking towards her. The same disconcerting sensation that had come over her on seeing Aiden the night before was back, this time with twice the force. Her dismay showed on her face.

'What's wrong?'

'That's my fiancé's sister coming this way. She doesn't like me and she's never needed an excuse to do a bit of stirring.'

'Does she know that we used to be together?'

Helen shook her head. 'My fiancé knows but it's not exactly the kind of thing you advertise to your future in-laws.'

'Then what are you worried about?'

'I don't know,' snapped Helen. 'She'll find a way to twist things and make this into something it's not. That's what she does. It's like her superpower.'

'Leave it to me,' said Aiden. 'Just keep making out like we're having a casual chat and I'll do the rest.'

While not exactly enamoured of the idea of leaving anything in Aiden's hands, Helen didn't exactly have a choice other than to beg Caitlin for mercy and so she allowed Aiden to ramble on about how nice the weather was while every now and again making inane weather-based observations of her own until Caitlin was within earshot.

' . . . well I'd really like you to give it some consideration,' said Aiden loudly, 'but obviously I need someone quickly so the sooner you can make a decision the better.' He stopped and looked directly at

Caitlin, which Helen assumed was her cue to turn around.

'Caitlin,' said Helen brightly. 'What are you doing here? Aren't you meant to be having lunch?'

'I was about to say the same to you. One minute you were there, the next you'd disappeared and no one seemed to know where you were, so I thought I'd come out and make sure you were okay.'

Aiden held out his hand. 'My fault entirely. The name's Aiden. Aiden Reid.'

'Hi,' said Caitlin coolly, 'pleased to meet you. So how do you know Helen?'

'We used to work together a long, long time ago.'

'Really? What a coincidence, the two of you being here at the same time.'

'I'm actually here for a friend's stag weekend – you might have heard of him, Karl Peters?'

Caitlin's eyes widened. 'You mean Karl Peters off the TV? Then . . . you . . . you can't be! You're not *the* Aiden Reid are you?'

'I am indeed,' replied Aiden.

It was obvious to Helen that Caitlin had known exactly who Aiden was the moment she laid eyes on him. And equally obvious that Caitlin wasn't the slightest intimidated by his fame. Caitlin had simply chosen to appear star struck because she thought it would flatter his ego.

'Helen Richards, I can't believe you!' said Caitlin. 'All these years and you've never once mentioned that you used to work with Aiden Reid. I'd be bragging about it to everyone I met.'

It was, thought Helen, possibly one of the finest acting performances she had ever seen. Caitlin was positively oozing faux naïve charm and had she not seen first-hand what her sister-in-law-to-be was capable of, even she might have fallen for it.

'I was just bending her ear about my show,' continued Aiden, 'and Helen made such perceptive comments that I think that she'd be right for my production team. I need someone good at the top and Helen could be it.'

Caitlin turned her gaze to Helen. 'Are you going to take it?'

'I said I'd think about it.'

'Right,' said Aiden, 'I'm supposed to be playing golf with the boys so I'd better get off but hopefully I'll bump into you guys later. See you soon?'

'Yes,' replied Helen, searching Aiden's face for meaning. 'I guess you will.'

10.

Before Helen could spend even a fraction of a second contemplating the complexities of this conversation Caitlin interrupted her, seemingly fired up by her encounter with a celebrity.

'I can't believe I've just met Aiden Reid!' she squealed in an uncharacteristic fashion. 'And he's such a nice guy too. Did you really used to work with him?'

Helen wished Caitlin would drop her act, but she had to be careful not to rile Caitlin so much that she took it upon herself to start asking questions of Phil.

'For a couple of years yes,' said Helen. 'He was a nice enough guy when I knew him.'

'But you don't like him now?'

'I don't know him now. It's been a long time since I've had anything to do with him.'

'But he seems lovely. And him offering you a job, well you must be thrilled. I'm sure it would be much better being a small fish in a big pond, especially working with someone of Aiden's calibre. You should definitely take it. Think how glamorous it would feel after having spent so long entertaining the kind of people who usually listen to your show – no offence, obviously – but you know what I mean.'

'None taken,' said Helen wearily. 'I'll bear it in mind.' Helen hoped that this would be the end of the conversation and that they might travel the last few hundred yards to the restaurant in a comfortable silence but it wasn't to be.

'He's not still married is he?'

'I don't know,' lied Helen. 'I don't make a habit of keeping up to date with the love lives of people I used to work with.'

Caitlin didn't get the joke. 'Still, he's different isn't he? I mean he's a proper celebrity. Who was he married to again? I can see her face and her name is on the tip of my tongue. It's Sara something . . . or Sonya . . .'

Helen felt like screaming. 'Sanne. Her name was Sanne.'

'That's the one!' exclaimed Caitlin. 'Sanne! She was in that girl band wasn't she? They had that updated Dusty Springfield cover? Very beautiful as I remember. Absolutely stunning in fact. I'm guessing you don't know why they split up?'

'No idea.'

Caitlin wouldn't let it go. 'I'd call my friend Beth and ask her because she's practically got a PhD in celebrity gossip but she's on holiday in Bahrain at the moment.'

'That's a shame,' said Helen drily as they finally reached the restaurant. 'Maybe you should call her anyway. It seems an awful waste to have that much knowledge and miss out on the chance to use it.'

Helen made a beeline for her friends hoping to get rid of Caitlin as soon as was humanly possible but unfortunately now that Caitlin had Aiden on her mind it was apparent that she was reluctant to be offloaded.

'You'll never guess who Helen and I just bumped into,' said Caitlin excitedly as Helen closed her eyes and concentrated all her latent psychic abilities on persuading the earth to open up and swallow her whole. 'Aiden Reid.'

Revealing hitherto unknown amateur dramatic skills the girls sounded totally convincing in their shock and surprise. Helen opened her eyes and as she did so she caught Yaz's gaze and her friend mouthed a silent 'Sorry' across the table.

Caitlin gave the table a blow-by-blow account of the conversation documenting everything from the exact colour of his eyes through to the precise tone of his voice when he'd said goodbye.

'You almost sound like you've got a bit of a crush on him,' teased Kerry.

'I think he quite fancied me actually,' said Caitlin without a moment of self-awareness, 'but he's not really my type.'

Helen stood up. She'd had enough and didn't care who knew it.

'Of course!' said Caitlin, 'you must be starving and here's me yakking on. I don't normally eat much at lunchtime beyond a bit of fruit so I don't really miss it, but I can imagine if you like your food, going without could really make you cranky.'

Too mentally exhausted to rise to the bait Helen headed to the buffet table and picked up a plate. As she tried to choose between a large dish of vegetable lasagne and the beef goulash next to it, Caitlin's 'if you like your food' comment echoed around her head and she put the plate down.

'I'm so pleased you did that,' said Caitlin behind her. 'Carbs at lunchtime are a real no-no and, well, don't forget we all want you to fit into that dress next Saturday!'

The last time Helen had punched someone she had been eight and the person she had hit had been her older cousin Sam. For reasons known only to himself while visiting from Southampton with his family, Sam had spent an entire morning teasing her, only to act surprised when she finally blew her top as he scribbled on her drawing of a castle. Helen lashed out with her right fist and connected perfectly with his nose, shocking herself so much by the act of violence and its effect (within seconds Sam's T-shirt was covered in blood) that she had never hit anyone since. As she looked into Caitlin's eyes and saw all the spite there she felt that same anger. Instead of making a fist, however Helen picked up a serving spoon, poked it fiercely into the lasagne, took out a huge scoop and then gave herself a scoop of the goulash *and* the chicken korma next to it, just daring Caitlin to say a word.

When Helen finally pushed away her plate (with half the food she had loaded on it still looking back at her), some of the girls had disappeared to get ready for the spa's trademark full-body detox – a ninety-minute beauty session involving dry skin brushing, the application of several different types of poultices and a head-to-toe seaweed mask. Helen's was happening in a short while and she was feeling both excited and apprehensive. The apprehension was due to the disclaimer at the bottom of the brochure: 'Please note that the full-body detox may cause some clients to feel overwhelmingly emotional. For this reason please refrain from drinking alcohol, remain hydrated and take time to decompress before and after attending your treatment.' What with her weekend so far, Helen was afraid she would start foaming at the mouth the minute she walked into the therapy room.

With Caitlin less than two feet away, deep in conversation with Ros and Dee about the intricacies of Aiden's love life, there had been no opportunity for Helen to talk to Yaz privately, so when Yaz stood up Helen took this as her cue to make her escape.

'Listen,' said Yaz, as they stood by the French doors that led to the rear patio, 'I'm really sorry about dropping you in it earlier, but that is one sly cow you've got for a sister-in-law. I had my eye on her virtually the entire time as we came in to lunch and then there was a bit of confusion about what order the treatments were happening in, and by the time I'd sorted that out she'd gone. I thought about going after her but I was afraid of making things worse.'

'It's fine, really,' said Helen. 'Actually it was Aiden

who bailed me out in the end. He made up some story about wanting to hire me as a producer for his breakfast show but I think Caitlin was too busy flirting to notice how flaky it all sounded.'

'She was flirting with Aiden?'

'Uncontrollably. I've never seen her like it. Phil's always saying that because she's so pretty she tends to give most blokes short shrift. She normally goes for guys with good looks and money, investment banker types and she even makes them work pretty hard. But you should have seen her with Aiden: she was practically all over him from the minute he said hello.'

Yaz laughed. 'Not that I know him but I'm guessing she's not exactly Aiden's type.'

Helen shrugged. 'You'd hope not, but nothing would surprise me with those two.'

'So what did he want?'

Helen rolled her eyes. Where to begin with that one? 'Do you know what? I really have no idea. He was insistent that we went for a walk and took me to this really pretty spot down by a stream and started rambling on about how great it was to see me, how he thought my show was good. Then I finally plucked up the courage to tell him that this is actually my hen weekend and he seemed to go a bit weird.'

'Weird how?'

'Well, put it this way, the last thing he said to me before her royal highness turned up was that the reason he split up with his ex-wife was because of me.'

'Because of you? But that doesn't even make sense!

You hadn't even seen him since you two split up!'
Helen looked guilty. Yaz was incredulous. 'Are you
saying that you'd seen him before today?'

'It was just the once, I swear,' said Helen. 'About five
years ago he contacted me out of the blue basically
begging to meet up.'

'So you said yes? Are you mad?'

'I must have been,' sighed Helen, 'because when I
look back the whole thing was more like a dream than
reality. We met, we talked, he apologised for the way
things ended and then we went our separate ways. It
was all over in under an hour. I remember thinking to
myself, "Did this really happen?" '

'And you never told Phil?'

'What would have been the point? I knew I wasn't
going to get back with him.'

'So why did you see him?'

'Because I wanted to show him that he hadn't
crushed me. I wanted him to know that I'd moved on.'
She laughed bitterly. 'Maybe that's what he wanted too
because less than a week later his girlfriend was in all
the papers showing off her engagement ring.'

'And now he's blaming you for the marriage not
working out because, what, he was still in love with
you?'

'I don't know. None of it makes sense.'

Yaz considered the situation for a moment and was
ready to dispense her advice: 'Seems to me that you've
got two choices,' she began: 'one, you can spend the
rest of the weekend driving yourself crazy trying to

work it out or two: go and ask him. You can't just leave it like that, H, you know you can't.'

'I'm not so sure,' said Helen. 'How would I even bring the subject up and more to the point, do I really want to know?'

'So you're just going to leave it?'

Helen shrugged. 'For now I'm just going to do everything I can not to think about it.'

A combination of Yaz immediately having to dash off for her full-body detox, the lure of the outdoors thanks to the strength of the summer sun, and Helen's head beginning to ache meant that for the time that she had left before her beauty appointment she did nothing other than grab her things from her room and lie on one of the loungers flicking through a copy of *Harper's Bazaar*.

She looked at her watch. It was time to go. She grabbed her tote bag and headed across the grass to the Spa.

At the spa reception Helen was handed a clipboard with a form covering everything from her health to her current state of mind. Normally Helen hated filling out forms but as this was more like a quiz in a women's magazine than a tax return she filled it in with gusto.

A few moments later a troupe of young, white-uniformed girls arrived at reception and called out the name of their individual clients. Helen's was a pretty auburn-haired girl who introduced herself as Roisin whom Helen warmed to straight away.

The lights in the treatment room were dimmed, a tall

scented candle was burning on one of the white marbled surfaces and 'new age whale music' was coming from a slim-line iPod speaker. Roisin handed Helen a robe and promised to return once Helen had undressed.

'Right, let's have a look at your details,' she said picking up the clipboard. Her accent was strong and northern. Preston or possibly Stockport, thought Helen, definitely not Manchester.

Roisin sat down opposite Helen, double-checked her form and then set it down on a side table.

'Right,' she began, 'now we can get on with the business of getting you detoxed!' She looked into Helen's eyes. 'So that I can tailor the treatment to your exact needs I need a little bit more information. First off: how would you like to feel at the end of this session: energised or relaxed?'

'Relaxed,' said Helen quickly.

'I could tell!' joked Roisin and then she put her hand to her mouth. 'I'm sorry. I shouldn't have said that.'

'Don't be daft,' said Helen. 'You're fine. I'm not surprised I look stressed. I *am* stressed.'

'Oh no,' said the girl, 'you don't looked stressed. Well, no more than any of the other ladies who come here. I could tell . . . well I could tell from your *aura*.'

'My aura?'

'I'm in training to be the spa's reiki specialist and the minute I saw you in reception your aura just jumped out at me.'

Helen frowned. 'That doesn't sound good.'

'It's not, to be honest. It's very negative. But don't worry, there are oils we can use to cleanse it.'

'You're saying my aura needs cleansing? What's wrong with it? I haven't damaged it, have I?'

'It's hard to say,' replied Roisin. 'People usually get a negative aura when they're at a crossroads and don't know which way to go. When I left college at eighteen and didn't know whether to go into hairdressing or carry on with beauty therapy, I went to a reiki healer and they said the same about my aura.'

'And they fixed it?'

'It took a few sessions but yeah, it was okay in the end.'

Helen felt her stomach flip over. She didn't believe in any of this stuff. In her time on the radio she'd interviewed countless healers, exorcists, white witches, new age practitioners and clairvoyants and was always underwhelmed by how transparent their schemes were. And yet this girl seemed genuine, and as Helen reflected on her lack of a wedding dress, she began to wonder whether there might be something in it after all.

11.

'Right,' said Roisin as a comatose Helen lay face up on the therapy table naked but for her paper knickers and a long, thick white blanket-sized towel. 'I'm just going to step outside so that you can put on your dressing gown and then I'll take you to the post treatment room where you can have a lie down if you like before taking a shower.'

Helen stirred. This couldn't be right surely? An hour and a half couldn't have gone by just like that? The last thing she recalled was the girl applying a deep cleansing nutrient mask to her face. She reached up to feel if it was still there but there was nothing but the silky smoothness of her own skin. She opened an eye, tilted her head to look at the girl and with a not inconsiderable amount of panic in her voice said: 'It's not really over is it?'

'It is, I'm afraid. A lot of clients find that time really flies when they have this treatment. That's what happens when you're totally relaxed. Anyway, there's a glass of water on the counter and remember to sit up slowly.'

Sitting upright Helen recalled her troubled aura.

'How's my . . . you know?' she asked, a waggle of her eyebrows completing her sentence. 'Does it still look troubled?'

Roisin smiled. 'It's looking better, definitely. The oils I used took away quite a lot of the negative energy that was surrounding you but there's only so much you can do in one session. You need to look after yourself and try and relax more.'

'That's easier said than done,' sighed Helen.

'I know, but I guarantee you'll feel the benefit.'

As Roisin left the room Helen wondered whether she could justify booking herself another ninety-minute session straight away. She couldn't remember the last time she felt this good: her skin was smooth and supple, her muscles totally relaxed and her brain felt like someone had scooped it out and given it a warm bath before putting it back in place. What's more, she felt sure that whatever the problem with her aura had been before the therapy, Roisin had definitely dealt with it.

Gradually edging herself off the table, she wobbled enough to make her lean back against the table for support. It was the oddest feeling: her legs were weak but her body felt lighter than air. Slowly the strength returned to her limbs and as she began to get dressed she promised that no matter what the expense or inconvenience, the ninety-minute full-body detox would become a permanent fixture in her life.

Once Helen was robed Roisin led her down the corridor and through a side door into a darkened room fragrant with designer scented candles. There were several low beds (all empty) and each had its own table laden with bottled water and a small bowl of dried fruit and nuts.

'Feel free to stay as long as you like,' said Roisin. 'If you need anything or find yourself feeling light-headed just press the buzzer at the side of the bed.'

'Thank you,' said Helen sincerely. 'And I really mean that: thank you.'

'I'm just glad to have been able to help,' said Roisin reaching for the door handle. 'Enjoy the rest of your stay. And try and stay stress free.'

Helen looked down at the bed with its clean white sheets that looked so inviting. Feeling this relaxed, if she sat down to collect her thoughts she would fall deeply and embarrassingly asleep and so steeling herself she collected a set of towels from a table in the corner and made her way back to the changing rooms.

Showered and dressed but with her hair still wet, Helen made her way back towards the spa reception with a view to getting back to her room and squeezing in as much sleep as humanly possible before she would need to get ready for the evening ahead.

As she reached the spa reception she saw Yaz sitting in one of the comfortable chairs with her nose deep in a glossy magazine.

'Hello you,' said Helen. 'What are you doing here?'

'Killing time while I waited for you. Wasn't it amazing?'

'Incredible. Like nothing I've ever experienced.'

'Did you cry?'

Helen shook her head. 'Did you?'

'Just a bit but it was hard to tell whether that was the therapy or the fact that it was there bubbling under the surface waiting to come out anyway.'

The two women stepped outside into the late afternoon sun and both instinctively drew a deep breath and exhaled. Helen looked at Yaz.

'Are you okay?'

Yaz nodded and wiped her eyes. 'I'm fine, honestly.'

'You know you can talk about everything that's going on, don't you? Just because we're on this weekend doesn't mean you have to be the entertainment.'

'I know and thanks for saying that. But I'm okay. Just having a bit of a wobble, that's all. I probably shouldn't have done but I tried calling Simon earlier, just to say hello, and maybe see if we could talk for a while but the call went straight to voicemail.'

'The same happened to me when I tried Phil. I'm guessing their hotel has got really bad reception.'

'Or they don't want to be contacted.'

'Look, there's no point in speculating, is there?'

'I suppose not.'

Helen's heart sank as she looked up and saw Caitlin coming towards them.

'Oh great, just what I need to undo an hour and a half of ultimate relaxation.'

'Is it too late to pretend we haven't seen her?'

'Yes,' said Helen. 'Far too late.'

'Hi guys,' said Caitlin brightly. 'I'm so pleased I've

bumped into you because you'll never guess what just happened.'

'Why don't you surprise us?' said Helen wearily.

'Okay,' said Caitlin, 'it's like this. I was on my way for a swim before my treatment when who should be coming back from the golf course but Aiden Reid! We got chatting and to cut a long story short I invited him to dinner tonight and he's agreed. Isn't that amazing? Aiden Reid is coming to dinner with us!'

Helen held her breath as the familiar and unwelcome muscular tension and the headache returned. 'You did what?'

'I invited him to dinner. It's not a big deal is it? I was sure you wouldn't mind.'

Yaz stepped in. 'The thing is Caitlin, this whole weekend was meant to be a women-only thing, a chance for us all to relax, have a bit of a laugh and give Helen a good send off. If Aiden comes along tonight . . . I don't know . . . I just feel that it would change the atmosphere.'

'He's just one man,' said Caitlin rolling her eyes. 'I don't see what the big deal is. I doubt that he'd talk to any of the other girls anyway.'

Yaz's eyes narrowed. 'Meaning?'

'Oh, you know, Aiden's Aiden isn't he? No offence but given the lifestyle he's used to he won't be interested in a bunch of mums fawning over him all evening. I promise, I'll totally keep him under control.'

'But you're completely missing the—'

Helen interrupted. 'Leave it, Yaz, Caitlin's right. It's not that big a deal.'

'But—'

'It's fine,' said Helen firmly.

Yaz still wouldn't let it go. 'Are you absolutely sure?'

'Yes,' said Helen. 'I am.'

'Oh, that's absolutely brilliant,' said Caitlin kissing Helen's cheek. Helen couldn't believe it. Caitlin actually looked like she was almost grateful. 'Are you absolutely sure?'

'I've no doubts at all.'

'And you're not just saying that?'

Helen crossed her heart with the palm of her hand. 'Scout's honour.'

'You really are amazing do you know that?' beamed Caitlin. 'And I promise I'll make sure that he doesn't dominate the evening. I really think this could be the beginning of something good. Who knows, this time next year we could all be back here for my hen do.'

'I can't believe that just happened,' said Yaz as they stood watching Caitlin trotting down to the spa.

'If it was happening to anyone but me I might have actually found it funny.'

'How can she not have picked up on the fact that you don't want him around?'

'She picked it up all right,' sighed Helen. 'She just didn't care.'

'So why did you give in like that?'

Helen shrugged. 'I guess I'm just tired of fighting her.'

Frustrated and as angry with herself as she was with Caitlin, Helen suggested that she and Yaz have a drink on the terrace. They took a seat and ordered two gin and tonics.

'Do you know what?' said Helen as the waiter disappeared, 'I'm forever telling off listeners when they call in saying they hate this and they hate that because hate's a pretty strong term that shouldn't be used lightly but right now I do actually hate Caitlin. I know that sounds harsh but apart from the fact that she popped out of the same womb as Phil she has got no redeeming features whatsoever.'

'Do you think she really just bumped into Aiden or has she been stalking him the whole time?'

'Stalking. Definitely. Probably stalking while down-loading a document to her BlackBerry entitled: "How to hold your own when talking about golf" to give herself some conversational starters.'

'And that stuff about: "this time next year we could be here for my hen weekend!" I could've slapped her silly when she said that. Do you actually think she's serious?'

Helen shrugged. 'She's a pretty unstoppable force when she gets going and it's not like she isn't easy on the eye. I can't imagine Aiden really wanted to come to dinner though. Why would he go to all the effort of trying to talk to me if his intention was simply to wind me up?'

'Any more clues why he blames you for him and his wife splitting up?'

'I don't know,' said Helen, 'and I'm not sure I care. Anyway it doesn't matter whether or not he comes out tonight because I won't be there.'

'What do you mean?'

'Just that. I'm not coming. I'll be fine, Yaz. Tell the girls I've got some sort of bug and I want to get an early night in the hope of being better by the morning. They won't doubt it if you tell it right.'

'We can't go without you. It's your weekend. Why not just tell Caitlin that you've changed your mind about Aiden tagging along?'

'And have her looking daggers at me all night or worse still trying to work out why I'm so dead set against her getting together with him? No thanks. I might have to come clean Monday but right now I haven't got the energy. No, she can do what she likes. I don't care any more.'

'Then I'll stay too,' said Yaz. 'I won't enjoy the evening if I have to picture you crying into your soup. The others can go, we'll stay and maybe treat ourselves to a few items off the à la carte menu. How does that sound?'

'If you don't go none of them will and I'll feel obliged to entertain them all evening which is frankly the last thing I need.'

The waiter arrived with their drinks and the two friends fell into an uneasy silence. A young couple (clearly very much in love and celebrating an anniversary) sat down at the table next to them. The man reached across for the woman's hand and her whole being lit up. Helen could see that Yaz was thinking the same thing: how wonderful that stage of a relationship was and why did those feelings all too quickly fade.

Helen took a sip of her drink. 'I'm going back to my room.'

'Are you sure about later?'

'One hundred per cent.'

'The girls will be devastated.'

Helen smiled. 'They'll be fine, if you keep them distracted.'

The two women hugged.

'You take care okay?' said Yaz. 'And if you need anything, just call me.'

Reaching her room, Helen lay down on the bed and closed her eyes. It felt good to be out of the sun for a while and the cool of her air-conditioned room seemed to take away the residual anger that she had felt towards Caitlin. Now she was able to pity her, as she would any human being so full of resentment they couldn't see the good in anyone.

Helen took out her phone and switched it on. There was a text from her boss asking if she was having a good time and another from a phone company offering a new phone deal but still nothing from Phil. Although rationally she knew better than to read anything into this continuing lack of communication, she couldn't help but conclude that whatever else he was doing at this particular moment, he wasn't thinking about her and in this post-detox emotional state this almost reduced her to tears.

The only way forward was to distract herself. She switched on the TV and started flicking around the channels and was relieved when she came across the

film *All About Eve*, easily her favourite Barbara
Stanwyck movie. Drawing the curtains, she made
herself a cup of tea and climbed underneath her duvet
to watch the film and there she remained for the best
part of an hour until there was a knock at the door.

Helen's first instinct was to ignore it, but when the
knocking persisted she opted to answer it on the off
chance it was an emergency.

Helen grabbed a towelling dressing gown from the
bathroom door and was still tying the belt around her
waist as she looked through the peephole and saw
not just one face but many looking back at her. It was
the girls.

'I tried to tell them you were ill,' explained Yaz
plaintively as they flooded into Helen's room. 'But I
don't think they bought it.'

'Listen girls,' said Helen sitting on the bed as they
all surrounded her. 'Don't think this show of solidarity
isn't appreciated, but as I said to Yaz earlier, I'm not
interested in battling with Caitlin. She's a mean,
hard-hearted cow who needs taking down a peg or
two but that doesn't mean that I have to be the
person to do it.'

'All that's fine,' said Heather, 'but why does she get
to spoil your hen weekend just because she's Phil's
sister?'

'Heather's right,' chipped in Ros. 'We came here for
you this weekend. There's no way Caitlin should be
dictating proceedings.'

'I know it's not ideal,' began Helen but so many of

127

the girls added their voices to the protest that she couldn't be heard.

'The fact of the matter is this,' said Heather, 'we'd rather stay in our rooms and not go out at all than go out without you.'

Helen looked to Yaz for some support but Yaz shook her head. 'Don't look at me,' she said grinning. 'I'm with them. I don't want to go to some posh restaurant without you. It wouldn't be the same.'

Helen surrendered. If she had been feeling despair an hour earlier, then this was the complete opposite. All these old friends, all their good will, it really meant something. There was no way she could turn them down.

'Okay, okay, I'll go,' she said grinning. 'But if that scrawny cow so much as looks at me funny I can't guarantee that I won't smack her one.'

'Don't worry,' said Yaz, 'if she does anything wrong you'll have to join the queue to get to her.'

12.

Helen knocked on the door to Yaz's room so that they could go down to reception together. Although the prospect of the evening ahead filled her with dread, little of it was due to Caitlin. Yes, Caitlin would be her usual mean-spirited self but it was Aiden's presence that truly set her on edge. No good would come of him sharing whatever was on his mind and while her natural curiosity was piqued she determined to override it. Her mission tonight was simple: avoid Aiden.

Yaz looked amazing in a black top with chiffon sleeves and black trousers and Helen told her so.

'You look great too,' she said, admiring Helen's outfit. Helen had been uncertain about diverting from her usual smart trousers and top combo in favour of a dove grey soft drape dress teamed with strappy heels. It was, she was aware, more of a sexy look than was her usual and this had been exactly why she had bought it to wear for the meal tonight, knowing that surrounded by her closest friends, she wouldn't have to feel self-conscious. But Caitlin inviting Aiden to the meal had changed everything. Now Helen was veering between defiance that she had every right to dress the

129

Mike Gayle

way she wanted, to anxiety that her choice of clothing would send out the wrong signals. Decades of feminism and the supportive comments of her friend eventually won over. 'Phil is the luckiest man in the world getting to come home to you every day.'

The moment she heard Phil's name Helen's stomach tightened into a ball. Much as she resented this neediness that seemed to have bubbled up from the depths of her subconscious, she really did wish that he had called her back. His lack of communication was yet another issue for her already overstretched emotional resources.

The two women made their way over to the meeting place over loud applause from the rest of the girls, much to the hotel staff's amusement. There was no sign of Catlin yet and so seizing the opportunity Helen called over one of the porters, handed him her camera and asked him to take a photo of them. As the flash went off Helen knew even without seeing the evidence that what had been captured was a proper Kodak moment: all of her oldest, closest friends gathered together in one spot ready to have a good time. A rare thing and something to be treasured.

The girls were all still cackling and making outrageous comments to the porter as Caitlin emerged from the lift.

'What did I miss?'

'Nothing,' replied Helen quickly. 'We were just messing about, that's all. You look great.'

Caitlin smiled but there was no compliment in return.

130

She glanced around the lobby clearly looking for signs of Aiden but didn't say as much to Helen.

'What time are the cabs booked for?'

'About now,' said Helen.

Caitlin nodded. 'Right, we'll I'm just going to check my make-up. I'll be back in a minute.'

Helen was tempted to herd the girls into a cab the moment she was gone but before Caitlin had taken a step Aiden appeared at the top of the stairs. He was wearing a black suit and tie matched with a white shirt that instantly recalled Phil's Reservoir Dog outfit. Helen swallowed hard. It was as if the universe was doing all it could do to tip her over the edge.

'I'm not late, am I?'

'No,' said Helen. 'You're right on time.'

He kissed her on the cheek. His skin felt soft and his aftershave smelt light and citrusy. She closed her eyes and breathed deeply. She determined never to get that close to him again.

Caitlin moved expectantly into his orbit and Aiden kissed her too. Helen glanced at her watch. How was she ever going to get through this night when it already felt like it had gone on too long?

Aiden smiled. 'Are you sure you're okay with me coming tonight?' he asked. 'I'm sure these things are usually girls only but Caitlin here was very insistent.'

'Of course,' said Helen graciously. 'The more the merrier. Although shouldn't you be out with your friends?'

131

'I said I'd catch up with them later. Things never really get going with that lot until the early hours.'

Helen looked at her watch again and peered outside. There were two limousines parked outside but no sign of the taxis Yaz had ordered. 'I'd better go and check on the cabs,' said Helen. 'It looks like they're running a bit late.'

' 'Fraid not, fella,' said Aiden. 'They're not coming.'

'And you'd know this because?'

'I sorted those bad boys out front by way of an early wedding present instead.'

Shocked, Helen stepped forward to take another look at the limousines. With their blacked-out windows they were the kinds of cars celebrities emerged from looking radiant at red carpet events. This was so typical of Aiden. Big gestures had always been his thing.

'It's very kind of you,' she said. 'But it's too much, Aiden. We'll be fine as we are.'

'Too late,' he replied. 'They're paid for and you've got them for the night.'

'You'll have to forgive my sister-in-law,' said Caitlin sidling closer to Aiden. 'She's just not used to the high life. They are fantastic, and it's a lovely gesture. Of course we'll take them.'

'Plus,' said Aiden guiltily, 'I've already cancelled your other cars so I'm afraid you're stuck with them.'

Helen sighed. She hadn't even left the hotel and already the evening was turning weird. Why was Aiden trying so hard with her? Was it guilt or was there something more?

'What's going on?' asked Yaz. 'Everything okay?'

Helen gestured to the limousines. 'Grab your stuff, girls. Looks like we've just been upgraded.'

Helen had been desperate to visit their destination for the evening, the Michelin starred restaurant La Salle de Classe ever since she had read rave reviews of its opening in several Sunday newspapers at the beginning of the year. Around her birthday she had hinted to Phil that he should take her there but despite many lovely gifts and surprises from her fiancé (although she had to admit the La Perla underwear he had bought that was two sizes too small had gone down like a lead balloon) the big day had come and gone without the requisite visit. So when Yaz had asked for ideas about restaurants for the second night of the hen weekend Helen got out her laptop and typed the name and its address into Google Maps. Once she was sure that the journey was doable in a taxi, she gave the details to Yaz with orders to book it straight away.

The journey to the restaurant was suspiciously incident free although it hadn't gone unnoticed by Helen that when she, together with Lorna and Kerry, had climbed into the first car, Aiden had climbed in straight afterwards quickly followed by Caitlin. For most of the journey Caitlin locked Aiden into her conversational orbit leaving Helen to chat with her friends while exchanging increasingly excited texts with the second car following behind. Every once in a while Aiden attempted to break free of Caitlin and join

Helen's conversation, but even his extensive verbal skills were no match for Caitlin, and with a surgical skill that betrayed her borderline sociopathic tendencies she made sure that the conversation came back to her and only ever had two participants.

It was just after eight o'clock as the limos pulled up in front of the large plate glass windows of their destination.

'What's this place like?' asked Aiden peering into the packed restaurant. 'Anyone eaten here before?'

'I think it's new for all of us,' replied Helen. 'But I for one can't wait to get inside.'

The décor of La Salle de Classe was as high end as its food and as she waited to be seated Helen fell in lust with so many of the fixtures and fittings that had she possessed a screwdriver and a much larger handbag some of the items she coveted would have quickly been liberated.

As the maître d' arrived to show them to their table Yaz took control of the seating plan. Helen as guest of honour was at the head of the table with Yaz on one side and Heather on the other, whilst Aiden and Caitlin were tucked at the opposite end as far away from Helen as possible. Carla, Ros and Heather set the tone for the rest of the evening by ordering champagne to toast the bride to be.

The meal was stunning and Helen found herself enthusing about the beetroot and caramel sauce on her wild sea bass long after the waiter had handed out the dessert menus.

The girls had done such a good job of keeping her wine glass topped up and entertaining her with stories from the past that she had barely taken any notice of Caitlin and while Aiden had once or twice tried to attract her attention, she had so far managed to avoid making eye contact. As the waiter cleared away the dessert plates and took coffee orders she began to feel that she was home and dry.

It was at this point that her plans started to unravel. Some of the girls began talking about the next stage of the evening, given that it was only half past ten, and a consensus began to form that the only fitting conclusion to the evening would involve going on somewhere else. Helen tried to hint that she wanted to go back to the hotel but the girls were so emboldened by alcohol that the idea assumed a life of its own with suggestions ranging from heading to the nearest wine bar through to going clubbing in Buxton's one and only nightclub. In the end a compromise was struck; they would go clubbing but not in Buxton and after half an hour of Aiden making various calls to people in the know, they got back in the limousines and made the fifty-minute trip to a Manchester club where he had got them on the guest list.

Helen knew all she had to do to put a stop to this madness was play the 'It's my party card' and the girls would fall into line. She didn't want to go clubbing at all and certainly not in Manchester with her ex-boyfriend and her borderline insane future sister-in-law. But her friends were having such a good time that she found herself saying feebly, 'Okay, if we aren't back too late.' Before she could change her mind, a club hits CD was on the sound system and a bottle of champagne from the car's drinks cabinet was being popped open.

By the time the limousines pulled up in front of Koko's, on the south side of Manchester city centre, a combination of the champagne and the long car journey had left Helen feeling slightly nauseous and she couldn't wait to get out of the car. The fresh summer air cleared her head and as she saw just how excited her friends were she resolved to enjoy herself after all.

According to Aiden, Koko's was Manchester's most exclusive club and the number one destination for the city's beautiful people. Helen cared less about Manchester's beautiful people than she did about whether or not she would be able to dance to the music. It had been a long while since she had enjoyed a good dance and even longer since she had been out clubbing and the last thing she wanted was to have this sterling opportunity frustrated by a DJ playing anonymous dance music.

Reassured that the DJ was one of the country's best they all followed Aiden past the door staff and straight to the club's VIP section where three bottles of champagne were waiting on ice.

'Was this your doing again?' asked Helen as they all sat down.

Aiden shrugged nonchalantly. 'My only concern this evening, my lady, is that you have a good time.'

Before Helen could respond Caitlin appeared at Aiden's side and dragged him over to Heather and Ros under the pretext that they were desperate to hear more of his celebrity stories.

Aiden flashed Helen a look of apology that she felt obliged to acknowledge. Even Helen could see that whatever her future sister-in-law's attractions, he was paying too high a price for the privilege.

Helen rounded up those of her friends that were up for a dance and led them to the dance floor just as the DJ played a track that seemed to be so well known that the whole room erupted. Helen had never heard it before, but with her friends by her side and the champagne flowing through her veins she didn't care. Tonight was her hen night and she was going to have a good time no matter what.

'I know it's all been a bit mad,' slurred Yaz, knocking back the last of the drink in her hand and lighting up a cigarette as they stood looking out across the city on the club's outside terrace after a solid hour on the dance floor, 'but you have to admit it's been an absolutely amazing night. Beats my Blackpool bash hands down!'

Helen kissed her intoxicated friend's glowing cheek. 'I don't remember you complaining too much.'

'You know what I mean,' said Yaz. 'It's been brilliant hasn't it?'

Helen nodded. 'It's like we're all twenty-one again! Last week I would've put good money on us all being in bed by now. It's fantastic.'

'And Caitlin's not ruining it for you?'

Helen plucked Yaz's cigarette from her hand and took a deep drag. 'She's good,' replied Helen, savouring the smoke in her lungs before exhaling, 'but not that good.' She handed the cigarette back to Yaz. 'I'm just grateful that you talked me into coming. It would have been awful if tonight hadn't happened just because of her.' She hugged Yaz. 'You, my lady, are easily the best friend a girl could have. Someone should clone you so that everyone can have one.'

Yaz laughed and then shivered. 'It's colder than you think,' she said rubbing her bare arms. She took one last drag on her cigarette and stubbed it out. 'I'm going back inside. Coming? I'm gasping for a drink.'

'Are you sure you haven't had enough? You've been knocking it back since we got here. Why don't you give it a rest?'

'What for? So I can spend the rest of the night thinking about what Simon's up to in Amsterdam? No thank you very much! I'll take being clattered over being sober, clattered is good, sober is just too much of a ball ache.'

Helen watched as Yaz turned and headed unsteadily down the stairs to the club. She thought about trying to talk her around but with everything going on in her own life, she thought Yaz had made a good point.

Helen turned her attention to the illuminated cityscape behind her. She loved imagining the lives behind the lights, lives she would never know, people she would never meet. It was like a visual representation of her job as a DJ.

138

Helen was lost in thought when she heard footsteps and turned around to see a young man standing in front of her. He looked to be in his twenties, tall and handsome and, judging from the surreptitious glances of some of the girls out on the terrace clearly something of a catch.

'Hope you don't mind me talking to you,' he said. 'You look miles away.'

'Got a few things on my mind,' said Helen.

He raised an eyebrow cheekily. 'Anything I can help with?'

Helen laughed. 'I doubt it.'

He held out his hand. 'The name's Paul but my mates call me Biz. Couldn't help but notice you on the dance floor earlier. You have one amazing body. Can I buy you a drink?'

'That's very kind of you . . . er, Biz . . . but apart from you being way too young for me . . . I'm actually getting married next weekend. So thanks but no thanks.'

'Well tell him from me he's one lucky guy.'

Helen smiled. 'They'll be the first words from my lips.'

He nodded, and gave Helen a wink. 'Knocked back by the pretty lady, you know you've broken my heart don't you?'

'You'll heal.'

He laughed. 'I probably will as well.' He offered a wave of his hand. 'You take it easy and have a good wedding, yeah?'

Grinning, Helen returned her gaze to the Manchester

streets. Chatted up by a hot young guy in a trendy nightclub! The girls were going to love this story.

She picked out a minicab snaking its way through the late-night traffic and tried to imagine who was in there and where they might be going. That was the key to being a good local DJ, being interested in people and their stories. It was true what Aiden had said about her ability to make something out of nothing. It was a skill that not everyone possessed.

Shivering slightly she rubbed her arms and was considering heading back inside when she saw the familiar figure of Aiden outlined against the night sky. Although she could barely see his face she knew he was looking at her. Every instinct told her to walk away but she didn't move.

13.

'Have you been out here long?'

'A little while,' said Helen. A group of young girls were pointing in Aiden's direction and sniggering, clearly having recognised him. 'Where's Caitlin?'

Aiden shrugged. 'She went off to powder her nose or whatever. It's cold out here. You must be freezing.'

'It's not that bad,' shrugged Helen, 'but I was going inside anyway. I'll leave you to have your cigarette in peace.'

Aiden held out a hand to stop her. 'I don't smoke,' he said. 'I told you the day my gran died I'd never smoke another cigarette and I haven't.'

Helen was flooded with shame. Aiden's gran had died of lung cancer in the third year they were together and losing her had affected him deeply.

'That's good,' she said. 'I'm glad you stuck to it.'

It was clear Aiden had other things on his mind.

'I came out here to find you,' he said as if daring her to challenge his assertion.

Helen didn't speak. Engagement in conversation was tantamount to encouraging him and that was the last thing she wanted to do.

141

'I'm out here because you've been avoiding me all night and I think I know why,' he continued.

Helen could no longer remain silent. 'Well, since we're here,' she said coldly, 'why don't you enlighten me?'

Taken aback by the sharpness in her voice Aiden held her gaze. 'I don't get it, why are you being so hostile? This can't be about your sister-in-law surely?'

Helen flushed with anger. 'Can you even hear yourself? You really think that nine years after you cheated on me I'm going to get upset because you're sniffing around that wannabe wag? Get over yourself! She could be moving into your penthouse and having your kids and I still wouldn't care. I can't think of two people who deserve each other more.'

Aiden put his hands in the air in an effort to placate her. 'Helen, please, just calm down for a second! I'm not interested in Caitlin. I thought you would have guessed that straight away. The only reason I accepted her invitation to come out tonight was because I knew it would be the only way that we'd ever get a chance to talk.'

'About what exactly?'

It was Aiden's turn to be indignant. 'Oh come on, don't play games, Helen. When I told you why Sanne and I split up I could see in your eyes that you wanted to know the reason why, but were scared to ask.'

'Well, if that was all so bloody obvious what are you even doing here? It's my hen weekend, Aiden! This time next weekend I'll have promised to be with the man I love for the rest of my life. Is this some kind of joke? A game where you waltz back into my life just because a very long time ago, we used to mean something to each other? I don't want to know why you split up with your wife. It has nothing to do with me.'

'You know that's not true. When you read about the divorce in the papers it must have been no surprise to you. Because you know the truth.'

'That you're a lying, cheating womaniser? I'm pretty sure everyone knows that truth.'

'Come on, Helen, you know me better than that. Why do you think I begged you to meet up all that time ago? Why do you think I got engaged? Why do you think it didn't work out with Sanne? It was all because I needed to prove to myself that I wasn't still in love with you.'

Helen shook her head in disbelief. 'That's such a lie! You didn't love me. You never loved me. If you did you would never have hurt me like that.'

'I just wasn't ready for that life.'

'Meaning once you'd hit the big time you didn't need a girlfriend!'

'It was never like that!'

'It was exactly like that! I chose you over my career and you knew that you would never be brave enough to do the same. That's why you cheated and that's why you're here because you've finally realised what I, and more than likely your ex-wife, have known all along. You're an emotional coward. You always have been and you always will be.'

143

'Fine,' snapped Aiden. 'Rage at me all you like, but it won't change a thing. I know you still have feelings for me. I know you still care. I know because my feelings for you haven't changed. The moment I laid eyes on you last night at the hotel it was like the last decade hadn't happened. Above all I know because I saw the doubt in your eyes when you told me you were getting married. You might think you love this guy and that might be enough to push you through but you'll never feel about him the way you felt about me. Never in a million years.'

Helen felt a surge of anger. She wanted to scream, she wanted to shout, she wanted to let out all the rage his arrogance and presumption had stirred up. But more than anything she wanted for him not to be right.

Pushing past him she ran across the terrace and back through the huge double doors into a wave of heat and sound that threatened to drown her. For a few moments she was lost in a sea of unfamiliarity, but as she slowly gathered her wits things began to make sense and once she spotted the tops of the bright red doors through which they had arrived, she headed for the exit.

The club was more packed than it had been. On the far side of the dance floor she could just about make out Carla and Ros although Caitlin and Yaz were nowhere to be seen. Helen began weaving her way around the edge of the dance floor but as she did so the DJ played yet another song that everyone in the club seemed to know and everyone flooded to the centre of the room taking Helen with them.

She almost lost her footing but quickly regained her balance and snaked in between dancing couples and groups of friends towards her destination. Every two inches gained seemed at the expense of one in the wrong direction as she struggled against the rising tide of happy clubbers. Finally she managed to break through when a group of girls dancing frenetically in front of her fell over. In the resulting commotion a few lads who had seen what had happened began holding people back and seizing her moment she dodged her way around them. She could almost see the edge of the dance floor when she felt someone grab her wrist. She turned around to see the young guy that had spoken to her earlier on the terrace. Grinning inanely he motioned that she should join him and his friends but Helen simply shook her head, wrenched her wrist free of his grip and continued on towards the exit.

There was one final obstacle to overcome before she reached the doors. A line of men, poseurs every last one of them, stood, drinks in hand eyeing up the talent. Helen bowed her head and barged right through them refusing to respond to or even acknowledge their comments as she did so. All that mattered was getting out. All that mattered was being somewhere safe.

As the large double doors closed behind her, muting the music, she stopped running so as not to attract the attention of the door staff. She left the club and scanned the street for any sign of the limousines that had brought them. There were lines of minicabs touting for business, but the limos were nowhere to be seen. Just as she was wondering whether she had enough money in her purse to cover the minicab fare if she could find one that would take her back to Ashbourne she heard Aiden's voice calling after her. She had slowed down too soon. Too exhausted to run any more she stopped and turned around.

Aiden walked towards her, encircled her in his arms and held her tightly to his chest. Overcome with emotion, Helen couldn't hold in her feelings any longer and as tears began to flow down her cheeks she looked up and melted into his kiss.

As they drew apart, Helen buried her face in his chest as if trying to block out the world and everything in it. She felt drained and longed to give in to the fatigue but a commotion outside the club demanded her attention.

'Looks like they're throwing out some trouble-makers,' said Aiden.

Helen shook her head. Even amongst the uproar she could pinpoint the voice of her best friend. 'It's Yaz, she's in trouble. She needs me.'

Helen ran back up to the door of the nightclub to find Yaz being manhandled by two of the door staff.

'What's going on?'

'What's it to you, love?' asked the taller of the pair.

Aiden stepped forward. 'Listen guys, this is a close friend of mine. Is there anything I could do to help sort out the problem?'

'She was being abusive to the bar staff, Mr Reid, and she made the whole thing worse by taking a swing at one of them. At this establishment we have a zero tolerance policy towards violence directed at staff members.'

'I just wanted a drink and the bastards wouldn't serve me,' slurred Yaz, attempting to wrench her arms from the door staff's grip.

Helen and Aiden exchanged wary glances. 'She's just split up with her husband,' explained Helen. 'I knew she was drinking a lot but I never guessed she was this bad.'

Aiden nodded and stepped towards the more talkative of the two doormen. 'Listen guys, you haven't called the police have you?'

'Not yet. We were just deciding what to do.'

'How about this,' said Aiden, 'you let her go and I promise that she'll never come here again. What's the name of the person she took a swing at?'

'Dave.'

'Right, well first thing in the morning you get Dave to give me a ring on this number,' Aiden scribbled his number down on a piece of paper and handed it to the man, 'and I'll make sure he's looked after. That means coming down to London, dropping into the show and putting him and a mate up in a nice hotel. What do you say?'

The two exchanged glances and the taller one replied. 'Okay, Mr Reid, but only because it's you. You do need to get her out of here pronto though.'

The door staff let Yaz go and she ran to Helen and started to cry.

Aiden pulled out his phone and made a call to the

limousine driver. 'He's just around the corner,' said Aiden. 'They'll be here in a minute. You get the rest of the girls together and we'll head back to Ashbourne.'

Helen tried Carla and then Heather but both times it went straight through to voicemail. She then tried Dee's number and breathed a huge sigh of relief when after three rings she picked up.

'Where are you?' asked Dee yelling over the din of the music. 'No one's seen you for ages.'

'I'm outside,' said Helen. 'Can you do me a favour? Just get the girls together as quickly as you can and then come out. We've got to go.'

The limousines arrived and Helen and Yaz climbed inside while Aiden waited for the rest of the group. They were there within a few minutes and he explained as tactfully as he could that something had happened and they needed to go. They all nodded and headed in the direction of the rear limousine but Caitlin, who was one of the last to emerge from the club, refused to move from his side.

'Where have you been?' she asked clinging on to his arm. 'I've been looking for you everywhere.'

'Look,' said Aiden, 'can you just get into the car?'

'What's going on?'

'Nothing's going on. Just go please.'

Obviously the worse for wear Caitlin bent down, looked into the limousine and locked eyes on Helen. 'Is this about her? Is something going on between you two?'

'Nothing's going on,' said Aiden. 'Just get into the other car will you.'

'Fine,' said Caitlin. 'But only if you come with me.'

Aiden shook his head. 'That's not going to happen.'

Caitlin's eyes narrowed. 'There is something going on. I can see it. I'm not stupid.'

'You can think whatever you like, Caitlin,' said Aiden. 'But it's probably worth pointing out that you're mistaken if you think anyone actually cares. And while it's up to you if you want to stand here talking to thin air all night, when I get into this car and tell the driver and his mate to go they will do exactly that even if it means leaving you stranded.'

Visibly shocked, Caitlin backed away from the limousine as Aiden got in, slamming the door behind him. Worried that she was about to leave her future sister-in-law marooned in a black sequined minidress in the middle of Manchester, Helen was relieved to see Caitlin disappearing into the second limousine.

The journey back to Ashbourne took place in silence with Yaz asleep on Helen's shoulder and Helen holding on tight to Aiden's arm the whole way. Every once in a while it would cross Helen's mind that she should clarify the situation in which she found herself, but she couldn't find the right words. It was too much of a task to choose the first one when she had an entire book's worth she wanted to say.

Arriving back at The Manor a little after half past three, Helen gave a little speech to the girls to the effect that everything was okay and it would all be explained in the morning, and they headed up to their rooms. Caitlin didn't look at Helen the entire time and was the first to leave the moment she was done. Helen didn't care. All she needed was sleep.

She helped Aiden take Yaz upstairs to her room.

'This is where we say good night,' said Helen. 'I can't leave Yaz on her own in this state.'

'Are you sure?'

Helen nodded.

Aiden moved to kiss her but Helen turned her face away.

'You'd better go,' she said.

'I'll see you in the morning.'

Aiden closed the door behind him, leaving her alone with a comatose Yaz.

Struggling with the dead weight of her semi-conscious friend, Helen tucked Yaz beneath the covers and, kissing her lightly on the forehead she sat down on the edge of the bed, put her head in her hands and wept.

Sunday

14.

Helen awoke with a start to hear the occupants of a nearby room having a loud conversation about the meal they had enjoyed the night before right outside her bedroom door.

She had returned to her own room in the early hours, leaving Yaz snoring soundly, and sat up until daybreak going over the events of the night, before crashing headlong into an exhausted sleep.

Reluctant to begin what she knew was going to be a difficult day she considered going back to sleep but then she looked at her watch. They were due to meet for breakfast at ten thirty and while she was sure that the majority of her friends were already regretting the decision, she at least ought to be there.

Checking her phone Helen noted the absence of any disappointment on seeing a blank screen but chose not to dwell on it. Setting the phone back on the bedside table she took a deep breath and reminded herself to take this day one moment at a time.

As she stood in the shower an image of her kissing Aiden flashed into her head and as she shuddered and pushed it out of her mind, it was replaced by the image of her clutching on to Aiden's arm in the back of the car on the journey back to the hotel. It was as though her subconscious was determined to review the events of the previous night even if her conscious mind was desperate to forget them.

Emerging from the shower, Helen switched on the TV to distract her while she dressed and put on her make-up. She wanted to go down to breakfast with Yaz and would miss her altogether if she didn't hurry up. Even though her hair was still damp she picked up her bag and keys, locked her door and made her way to Yaz's room on the floor below. She was about to knock when the door opened.

'Helen,' said Yaz guiltily, 'I thought you'd still be in bed.'

Helen looked down at the suitcase next to Yaz. 'What are you doing? You weren't planning on leaving were you?'

'Don't make a big deal out of it, okay?' sighed Yaz, 'I just have to go, that's all.'

'Without saying anything?'

'I was going to leave my car keys at reception and get a cab to the nearest train station.'

'But why? Not because of last night surely?'

'Of course because of last night! I made such an idiot of myself. I don't know what everyone must think of me.'

'They won't think anything.' Helen herded Yaz back into her room and closed the door. 'Please don't go.'

'But I need to. I've had enough of pretending my life's not falling apart when it so obviously is.'

'Fine,' said Helen. 'Then stop pretending. Everyone will understand. I know you're going through a lot at the moment. I understand that it must feel like it's all too much but that's why I want you to stay. I want to help.' She took Yaz's hand. 'You don't have to go through this alone. Whatever help you need, whenever you need it, it's yours.'

'But I've embarrassed myself. What was I doing drinking so much?'

'Oh, come on, babe, don't you think we've all been there? They'll be fine, I promise. And anyway, if we're talking about monumental cock-ups, your episode will be more than eclipsed by what happened to me: I've really messed up Yaz, I've messed up big time.'

'How?'

'I kissed him.'

'You did what? Why? How?'

Helen shook her head. 'I really don't know.'

Urged on by Yaz Helen told her everything that had happened with Aiden.

'So do you really still have feelings for him?'

Helen shrugged. The idea was too horrible to contemplate. 'I don't know. But I do know that I have had doubts about the wedding . . . about Phil . . . about everything . . . I haven't even bought my wedding dress!'

Yaz put her arms around Helen. 'And there was me worrying because I got lathered and took a swing at a barman!'

'So, we're agreed then,' said Helen raising half a smile. 'I am a total mess?'

'You're no such thing,' chided Yaz. 'Yes, you're in a difficult place but I know you Helen Richards – you'll find your way out.' Yaz tucked a stray strand of Helen's hair behind her ear. 'We're a right pair, aren't we? It's a wonder we can get out of bed in the mornings.'

'But we will be okay, won't we?' asked Helen.

'Of course we will,' said Yaz confidently. 'And if we're not, then at least we've got each other.' She stood up, checked her make-up in the mirror and looked back at Helen. 'You hungry?'

'I could murder a black coffee and toast.'

'Good,' said Yaz. 'Then let's go get breakfast.'

As Helen approached the girls' table it was obvious what they had been talking about. But she had given them a lot to discuss. All that mattered was that they were nice to Yaz and didn't ask too many difficult questions.

Thankfully, the girls were the very picture of discretion, making room for Helen and Yaz at the table, enquiring about how well they had slept but making no mention of the night before.

Helen poured them both coffee and checked out the girls' breakfasts. Although a few had opted for an English breakfast, most were tucking into a bowl of fruit, which made Helen think that her earlier decision to stick to toast had been a little rash. Mentioning as much to Yaz they headed to the bounteously laden breakfast buffet table.

Helen's spoon was hovering over a heaped serving bowl of raspberries and blueberries when she spotted

Aiden with his friends sitting on the far side of the restaurant.

Holding her gaze he got up and walked towards her.

'I didn't expect you to be up so early,' she said.

Aiden smiled. 'The lads want to get a good game in before we have to head off. Plus they were already mad at me for missing last night so I had to come down. How are you feeling?'

'Like someone ran over my skull with a lorry. You?'

'I'm okay. My hangovers tend to hit me about midday so not long to wait now. How's your friend?'

'Fragile.'

'But okay?'

'She'll be fine.'

'And has Caitlin said anything to you yet? I was pretty rude to her last night.'

'She had it coming. I'm guessing she's having breakfast in her room.'

'Have you eaten yet?'

Helen shook her head. 'You?'

'Just coffee. Why don't we get some food?'

Helen carried on filling her bowl with fruit while he helped himself to the constituent parts of an English breakfast.

They stood for a moment alternating glances between their respective tables. She could tell Aiden wanted her to sit with him but was wary of what signals such an action might send out, she was planning to return to her friends when he took her elbow and walked her over to an empty table.

As if struck dumb by the weight of so many eyes resting on them, they ate in silence for a few minutes until Aiden spoke: 'You know you can't go through with the wedding, don't you?'

'Let's not do this.'

'Do what? Not talk about the most important thing in our lives right now?'

Helen nodded. 'I can't.'

'I'm not saying run off with me. I'm not saying please leave him. All I'm saying is what you already know: you can't go through with this wedding.'

'You want me to call it off?'

'Not for my benefit. I'm trying to put the way I feel about you to one side. Right now I'm talking to you like a friend and no friend worth the job description would tell you that going through with this wedding would be the right move.'

Helen pushed her bowl away, glad to dispense with the pantomime of pretending she had any kind of appetite.

'I can't do that to him.'

'Of course you think you can't,' said Aiden. 'But that doesn't change the facts. You have to tell him the truth and you have to do it sooner rather than later.'

'It will kill him.'

'I'm not saying it'll be easy. But do you really have any option?'

'I wish I'd never seen you this weekend. I wish I'd just stayed home and locked all the doors.'

'You think that would have saved you?'

Helen thought about the wedding dress that she hadn't bought and bit her lip. 'Why does everything always have to be so complicated? Why couldn't Phil and I have just been happy as we were?'

'It's just the way life is, isn't it? Some get from A to B via the easy route and people like you and me . . . well we just take a little bit longer to get to where we're going.'

Helen stood up. 'I have to go.'

'What time are you off?'

'Some time after lunch.'

'We should talk again before you leave.' Aiden reached out and touched her arm. 'Are you okay?'

'No,' said Helen flatly, 'I'm not.' She made her way back to her friends and took a seat. In a transparent effort not to appear nosey the girls carried on with their conversation as if nothing had happened. Only Yaz acknowledged its significance with a brief meaningful glance.

The girls were discussing the third and final treatment of the weekend: Helen's wedding-day beauty preparation, a one-hour session in which the spa's top beautician and hair stylist offered Helen hair and make-up suggestions for the Big Day while the rest of them sat around and sipped glasses of complimentary champagne, ate handmade Belgian chocolates and bolstered her spirits. It was the girls' gift to Helen, the best way they could think of to see her off into her new life as a married woman. The more they talked about it, the more nauseous Helen felt.

'Are you okay?' asked Ros. 'You don't look very well.'

'I don't think I am,' said Helen. 'I think I might go for a lie-down before the treatment.'

Ros offered to take her back up to her room, but before she could even get to her feet Yaz was at her side holding her by the arm.

'It's no problem,' said Yaz quickly, 'I'll take her up.'

Helen could tell Ros knew that something was up but thankfully she made no comment. They arranged to meet at the spa later and made their way out of the restaurant.

'What happened? What did Aiden say?' asked Yaz the moment they were out of sight.

'Nothing I didn't already know. Everything's a mess, Yaz. Everything. How am I supposed to go through with that treatment feeling the way I do?'

'How do you feel? I'm not sure I know.'

'That's just it, that's how I feel: unsure. It would be so much easier if I could just blame all this on Aiden. It would be so much more straightforward. But the truth is, I was unsure before I even got here. I've been unsure since Phil brought this whole marriage thing up . . . Let's talk in my room,' said Helen, 'maybe if I tell you everything that happened again, we might be able to find a way out of this hole I've dug for myself.'

As they passed reception, there, at the desk, quite clearly checking out, was Caitlin.

Helen was hardly in the right frame of mind to deal with her sister-in-law and yet to leave Caitlin to her own devices would be to invite all manner of problems. She was probably contemplating contacting Phil to tell him everything that she knew if she hadn't done so already.

'I've got to speak to her,' said Helen as they reached the lift. 'Just wait here, and then I'll be straight back.'

She hadn't the slightest idea what she was going to say to Caitlin but she had to try.

The moment Caitlin finished checking out Helen walked over to meet her.

'We need to talk.'

'I've got nothing to say to you.'

'Please, this is really important.'

Caitlin turned away pulling her suitcase behind her. Helen followed her through the main doors to the steps outside. It was another bright and summery day, the sun was so strong that it felt as though she had stepped out of a black and white film into a Technicolor one.

'Caitlin, please!'

Caitlin continued down the steps so Helen ran ahead of her and stood in her path.

'Please, I'm begging you! Just stop!'

Caitlin went around her across the gravel towards the car park.

Angry with herself as much as she was with Caitlin, Helen called out after her: 'You go if it makes you feel better. You hated me from day one and you hate me now and that's never going to change.'

Caitlin turned around.

'I don't know what my brother ever saw in you.'

'Is that what this is about? That Phil made a decision without consulting you?'

161

'And a great job he's made of it!'

'What do you mean by that?'

'You know exactly what I mean,' spat Caitlin.

'And this is how you want this to end?'

Caitlin's eyes narrowed. 'You haven't seen the half of it.'

'Meaning?'

'Whatever you want it to mean. I'm done with you.'

'No,' said Helen, '*I'm* done with *you*. After nine years of putting up with your crap I'm going to give you a present that will make your day: the wedding's off. You win Caitlin. Phil is all yours! I hope the two of you are well and truly happy together.'

15.

Helen had no idea where she was going. Nothing mattered any more now she'd announced her decision. Leaving Caitlin open-mouthed on the driveway Helen headed back towards the hotel reception, before realising she couldn't face even Yaz, worse still, Aiden. So she headed towards the river mainly because it was the biggest thing on the horizon.

But reaching the river meant crossing the terrace and it seemed as though half the guests had come out to enjoy mid-morning refreshments. Helen ducked through an open French door that led to one of the lounges. She quickly composed herself and was about to go back outside when she saw some of Aiden's friends walking past the window and had to pretend to browse the bookshelf until they had gone.

Heading out of the lounge, Helen remembered the riverside space where she and Aiden had sat talking the day before. That was where she wanted to be. That was where she could be alone.

It was just as quiet as she remembered. The only sounds were the birds in the trees and the river flowing by, and within just a few moments of her sitting down the hot angry tears she had been holding back since her encounter with Caitlin finally burst through the dam that she had so painstakingly erected.

It was over. The nine years of loving and being loved by the one man in her life who had never done her wrong had come to a horrible conclusion, and the blame was all hers.

During her time with Phil, Helen's continuing fear had been that things would fall apart just as they had with Aiden. Despite trusting Phil implicitly, she couldn't stop worrying that he would meet someone else and end the relationship. In the many scenarios that populated her mind when at her most fragile it was never Phil who pursued these women but the women who pursued Phil. She imagined him out with his friends or at work and a woman who was more attractive or more understanding or who made him feel like his true self appeared in his life and would change everything.

There had even been times when Helen had found herself taking an irrational dislike to women Phil introduced her to who perfectly embodied her phantom nemesis. It didn't matter whether they were married or expressed less than zero interest in Phil while in her presence, if they fitted the bill and she could imagine Phil being happy with them then they were a threat. On rare occasions the jealousy would spiral out of control to such an extent that she would lock herself in the bathroom in the middle of the night frantically checking his text messages for evidence to lend weight to her theory. There was never anything of the kind. On the contrary: there was only evidence of his enduring love. Texts sent while he was away for work telling her that he loved her, jokey ones sent while she was on air telling her how sexy she sounded, thoughtful ones attempting to lift her spirits when he knew she was in for a bad day.

Helen felt shame when she remembered these moments and the shame was made so much worse by the fact that after all this anxiety and worry, she had been the betrayer rather than the betrayed.

She took her phone from her bag and looked at the screen. Still no sign of communication from Phil. If he had called, would it have made any difference to how the weekend had unfolded? Surely it would only have delayed the inevitable. Even so, she wished that she had heard from him. Hearing his voice would offer her some of the comfort she so desperately craved. Soon all that would change. Phil would hear about the events of the weekend and the next time she heard his voice it would be filled with hurt and anger. She longed to hear that voice filled with laughter and kindness one last time. She wished she had savoured those moments from the past, kept them safe for future reference. Instead, she had taken them for granted and now it was too late for anything other than regret.

Determined to bring her life back under control Helen made plans for the future. She would tell Phil about her misguided feelings for Aiden face to face and then move out. There were plenty of people she could stay with in the short term while she hunted for a place to rent and in the longer term she was convinced that if she cashed in her savings she would have enough for a deposit on a small place of her own.

Next she would call off the wedding. It would be too horrible and cruel to leave this to Phil. No, it would be her responsibility to contact all the guests and hers alone. A fitting punishment if ever there was one.

She would let Phil take the two-week-long honeymoon to Mauritius that had been one of the things he had organised so that he could have some time away. And depending on how much money she could lay her hands on, she would book herself a break somewhere warm where she could be alone to lick her wounds.

The only thing that Helen couldn't think about was Aiden. It was too soon and her feelings were too raw. She reminded herself that he wasn't the cause of this mess, merely a symptom and as such outside the circle of things that really mattered.

As Helen looked up through the leaf canopy above her head and felt the intense warmth of the sunlight on her face she felt grateful for the soothing silence. The real world felt a very long way off, too far away to harm her.

She heard a noise and looked up to see Yaz coming down the hill towards her.

'Finally,' said Yaz. 'You okay?'

'I'm fine,' said Helen. 'I'm sorry for being such a drama queen. Have you been looking for me for long?'

Yaz shook her head. 'When I came outside and there was no sign of you I went to the car park and there was

Caitlin loading her things into her boot looking for all the world like she'd been crying. I tried to ask what had gone on but she just snapped at me to speak to you and drove off. What happened?'

'I told her I was calling off the wedding.'

'But you didn't mean it surely?'

'I meant every word. Phil deserves better.'

'But there's no need for that. Maybe she won't tell him what happened.'

'She'll tell him all right and take great pleasure in doing so.'

'Well, that doesn't necessarily mean that Phil will want to call it off too. He really does love you, you know. You only have to see the two of you together. He won't give up on nine years just because you got cold feet.'

'I betrayed him.'

'You were confused.'

'Would you be so understanding if I were a man?'

'I'd say it no matter who you were.'

'I'm not sure I'd be so forgiving. Trust is everything to me.'

'But even the people we trust make mistakes.'

Helen shook her head. 'I don't think there's a way back from this. Some things are too bad, too awful to warrant forgiveness.'

'You're too hard on yourself.'

'That's just the thing. I don't think I'm being hard enough.' Helen closed her eyes. 'I think I might actually have feelings for him.'

Yaz could scarcely hide her shock. 'For Aiden?'

Helen nodded. 'You see? That's why I can't marry Phil.'

'I don't understand. When did this happen?'

'Maybe I've always felt this way on some level and just been too scared to admit it.'

'This is just your nerves talking,' said Yaz firmly. 'You've got cold feet about the wedding and Aiden has made it worse. I know you love Phil, and he feels the same way. You have to have faith in him, Helen, you have to have faith in yourself too, but more than that you have to have faith that love is enough.' Yaz put an arm around Helen. 'I promise you this whole mess will get sorted out somehow, just wait and see.'

With the late morning sun already high in the sky the two friends headed back to the hotel with the intention of checking out. Reaching the far edge of the hotel they gazed across the grounds taking in the full glory of their surroundings.

'We should come back here one day and do this whole thing properly,' said Helen solemnly as a flock of geese passed by overhead. 'No weddings, separations, sisters-in-law or anything else that might rain on our parade. Just me, you, and a weekend of high-end luxury.'

'I'll book it first thing, Monday,' said Yaz, 'but for now I think we should concentrate on just getting through today.'

It was twenty minutes to midday by the time Helen reached her room and surveyed all the work that needed to be done in order to check out on time. At the beginning of the weekend she had been scrupulous about packing dirty clothes away as she used them and generally keeping things organised and tidy but as time passed, her standards had dropped and her room looked like a bomb had hit it. There were dresses and tops spread over armchairs, underwear and swimwear on the floor and the entire contents of her make-up bag spread across the mirrored vanity table.

She opened her case, now largely empty, and made a start with the wardrobe, scooping all the items she had so carefully hung up there and unceremoniously dumping them inside before turning her attention to the floor. Within a few minutes she'd managed to cram more of her belongings in the case than there were scattered around the room but then she remembered the bathroom.

It took the best part of ten very frantic minutes to get everything done and as Helen stood surveying the room one last time she felt a pang of disappointment that this haven would no longer be hers. Soon the cleaners would come, strip down the bed and Hoover, sweep and dust away every trace of her existence ready for the next guest. Wishing the new occupants of the room better luck than she had enjoyed, Helen picked up her keys, left the room and closed the door behind her.

Most of the girls were already queuing up, wheelie suitcases and all, at reception. She joined the back of the queue behind an older guy who resembled an off duty rock star and his considerably younger significant other.

She wondered whether Aiden and his friends had checked out yet or whether, given their VIP status they had to check out at all, and were instead enjoying an early lunch or squeezing in a last-minute massage. Things were different if you had money. You could spare yourself the things that troubled the lives of mere mortals.

'Did you manage to bag all the toiletries?'

It was Yaz.

'All of them,' she nodded. 'You?'

'I couldn't fit in the conditioner or the moisturiser. I'm gutted.'

'Don't worry,' said Helen. 'I'll treat you for Christmas.'

'Any sign of you know who?'

Helen shook her head. 'I was just thinking about him actually.'

'In a good way or a bad?'

Helen sighed. 'Pretty neutral, considering.'

More members of staff arrived to help at reception and soon the queue had been dealt with and there was only Helen and Yaz left to check out.

Helen handed over her key and closed her eyes in anticipation of the bill. She began totting up some of the goods she had availed herself of that had seemed so reasonable at the time: several bottles of water at six pounds a go, numerous bottles of champagne, the twenty-pounds-per-bottle massage oil and the thirty-six-pounds-per-tub skin cream that she had asked the beauty therapist to add to her bill. She shuddered at all that wasted money and how long it would take to pay off her next overdraft.

She looked apprehensively at the receptionist.

'How much is it?'

The receptionist looked confused. 'Nothing. Your bill has already been settled.'

'There must be some mistake, I haven't—'

The receptionist looked concerned. 'Is there a problem? Mr Reid assured us that he had spoken to you about this.'

'Oh right,' said Helen quickly. 'It just slipped my mind. When did he sort this out?'

'About an hour ago.'

'Has he checked out?'

'I'm afraid I'm not authorised to give out that information.'

'Of course, I understand. I'll catch up with him later.'

She was surrounded by the rest of the girls.

'So come on then,' said Kerry, 'what was the damage? If it was anything like mine I bet it was a real killer! How they can charge sixteen pounds for a glorified tuna sandwich and keep a straight face is a complete mystery to me.'

'You should have seen mine,' added Lorna. 'When the bloke at reception handed it to me I nearly had a stroke. I said I'd only come for a weekend stay, not to buy the bloody place! Ian is going to do his nut when he sees the next Visa bill. Still, it's got to be a better use of our hard earned than flying out to Belgium for the weekend to watch motor racing in the rain.'

'So come on then,' said Kerry. 'How much was it?'

'More than I can afford,' said Helen. 'Much more.' She looked at Kerry. 'Could you do me a favour? Could you get all the girls together in the Silver Lounge? I think it's about time I explained what's been going on.'

16.

'So it's really, well and truly all off?'

Helen nodded. The sense of relief now that everyone knew was overwhelming.

'You poor thing,' said Carla giving her a hug. 'You've been completely put through the wringer.'

'I'm fine,' said Helen. 'Or at least I will be.'

'It is the right thing to do though,' said Heather. 'When I was younger and I broke off my engagement with Louis, it broke my heart at the time but it was absolutely the right thing to do. If I hadn't I'd never have met Wes, or had my lovely babies.'

Ros nodded in agreement. 'I know I'm not exactly the right person to be handing out advice given that I'm in the middle of a divorce but the only real crime would be to go through with it out of a sense of misplaced guilt. Of course it's sad, for you and for Phil but in the long term he'll appreciate you were looking out for him as much as you were yourself.'

'Thanks,' said Helen. 'I really appreciate all of your support. But the reason I gathered you all here is because I wanted you all to know that well . . . this whole weekend was supposed to be about us having a

173

good time and being really close when in fact I was doing everything I could to keep secrets from you.'

'It was a difficult situation,' said Heather. 'Anyway, most of us had guessed something was up and we knew you'd tell us when the time was right.'

Helen smiled. 'Bang goes my future with MI5. Anyway, despite everything, it has been amazing catching up with all of you and when the dust settles we should definitely put our heads together and come up with a good excuse for doing this again.'

'You're making it sound like you're off this very second.'

Helen looked guilty. 'That's because I am. I've got a lot of thinking to do before Phil gets back this evening so I thought it best to go now. I'll get a cab to the station, get a connection to Derby and then on to Nottingham.'

'You'll do no such thing,' protested Yaz and the others nodded in agreement.

'If you go,' said Ros, 'we all go.'

'Don't girls, please. The last thing I want is to ruin this weekend more than I already have.'

'Ruin the weekend?' laughed Dee. 'You have got to be kidding! A top hotel, relaxing beauty treatments, a Michelin-starred restaurant topped off with dancing until the early hours in Manchester! I'd pay twice the money for just half the fun.'

'She's right,' said Ros. 'I haven't laughed so much in ages. I wouldn't have missed it for the world. And while I know you're not putting it to the vote I don't think you should go home early either. We've still got lunch to look forward to, use of the spa and the swimming pool and while I understand that the bridal treatment we booked might not be appropriate right now, I'm sure they'd swap it for something else you'd enjoy. Just because the wedding isn't happening doesn't mean you don't need to treat yourself well.'

'You're not going to take no for an answer are you?' asked Helen wryly.

'Of course not,' replied Carla, 'we're sitting in paradise! This time last week I was being threatened with a broken beer bottle by a tattooed methadone addict who didn't like the fact that I was making her kids go to school! Frankly I'd handcuff myself to you for the rest of the afternoon if it meant we got to stay here an hour longer.'

'Fine,' said Helen, grateful to be surrounded by so many friends. 'I'll stay. I'd only sit at home and brood. So what now? The choice is up to you guys.'

'Let's check out the thermal pool that we passed on the way to the sauna,' said Ros. 'It's just a tiny covered pool with a bunch of lights stuck in the ceiling but it might be good for a laugh.'

'Or we could go back to the sauna,' said Ros, 'but we should use the plunge pool instead of chickening out like we did last time.'

'I felt the water,' laughed Yaz. 'It was bloody freezing!'

'We should do them all,' suggested Carla, 'and then this afternoon make out like we're posh nobs and hijack the croquet lawn and order afternoon tea. By the time we leave I want to really feel like we've exhausted everything on offer! I don't want to go back to north London! It's a ming hole compared to this!'

'So it's agreed,' chuckled Helen, 'thermal pool, followed by the sauna, followed by plunge pool, insert lunch somewhere in amongst the proceedings but make sure to leave enough time for croquet and cucumber sandwiches! I can already see they're going to have to call security to—'

Helen stopped abruptly.

'What's up?' asked Yaz. Caitlin was staring intently at them. 'I thought she'd left. What does she want now?'

'I'm not sure,' said Helen, 'but at a guess I'd say: round two.'

The Cross Keys was an old, stone-built, ivy-covered pub, the kind perfect for whiling away a lazy afternoon partaking of a traditional pint and Sunday lunch. Sadly, Helen wasn't there to while away an afternoon but rather to participate in her second confrontation of the day with Caitlin.

Caitlin bought the drinks (a mineral water for herself and a half of cider for Helen) and they made their way out to the beer garden which was heavily populated with locals enjoying the afternoon sunshine. There were no free seats so they followed the path down to the river and sat down on a wall overlooking the water.

Neither woman had said more than a handful of words since they had climbed into Caitlin's convertible, and as Helen took a sip from her glass she wondered if they were going to talk at all.

'What made you come back?' she finally asked, placing her glass down on the wall.

Caitlin shrugged. 'I felt bad. Truth is I have been a bit of a bitch to you from day one and you did nothing to deserve it. It wasn't fair. I never gave you a chance.' Helen felt dizzy hearing these words as though at any moment she might wake up and find herself in bed with a fever. 'The thing is,' continued Caitlin, 'I love my brother, Helen, I really do and he thinks the absolute world of you so I should have tried harder. I suppose what I'm trying to say is that I really wish you'd reconsider what you said today . . . I know there's nothing going on with you and Aiden and I should have known better than to have suggested otherwise . . . please don't call off the wedding. It would kill Phil if you did.'

'Is that what you're scared of? Phil blaming you if I call off the wedding?'

Caitlin shook her head. 'It doesn't matter why, does it? All that matters is not breaking my brother's heart. I'm begging you, Helen, don't call it off. Let's just put this whole thing behind us. We can do that, can't we?'

'I can't think of anything I'd like more, but it's just not going to be possible.'

'Because of me?'

'No,' said Helen. 'Because of me.'

'But Phil adores you.'

'I know,' said Helen. 'But I'm not sure it's enough.'

Caitlin looked bewildered. 'I know girls who would kill to have a guy like Phil in their lives.'

'So do I,' replied Helen. 'He's amazing. A truly wonderful man.'

'But?'

'I know you can never be one hundred per cent sure. I know that nearly all of life is a gamble. But the odds of us not working out feel too high.'

'It's just last-minute nerves.' It was ironic to hear Caitlin echoing Yaz. 'Have you tried talking to him?' she added cautiously.

'No,' Helen wondered if the stress in Caitlin's voice meant that she already had. 'His phone's been off every time I called. Have you managed to reach him?'

'I didn't try,' said Caitlin a little too quickly. 'It's not really my place is it?'

The words: 'Well, that's never stopped you before,' sprang to mind but Helen kept them to herself.

'So what now?'

'I go back to Nottingham and break the news to Phil when he gets home.'

'He'll be devastated.'

'He'll need all the support you can offer.'

'And there's no way around this?'

'None that I can see.'

'My mum was so looking forward to it.'

'So was mine. She'll be heartbroken.'

Caitlin stood up, defeated. 'I should get you back

before your friends call the police and tell them I've kidnapped you. I'm sorry this hasn't worked out.'

'Thanks,' said Helen. 'I appreciate that.'

It was a little after one by the time Caitlin dropped Helen off in The Manor's main car park. A number of people were loading up expensive looking cars with expensive looking luggage but there was no sign of Aiden and his friends.

'Are you sure you won't come and say goodbye to the rest of the girls?' asked Helen. 'They'll be sorry not to see you off.'

Caitlin smiled. 'I think we both know that's not really true.'

The two women embraced awkwardly before Caitlin climbed back into her car. Helen stood rooted to the spot as she reflected on everything she and Caitlin had been through. Would this be the last time they would meet? For better or worse Caitlin had been a part of her life for a long time and for her to disappear felt wrong. The thought that this might also be true for her and Phil made Helen's blood run cold.

Caitlin wound down her window and leaned out. 'Helen?'

'Yes?'

'Could you do me a favour?'

'Of course, what?'

'Tell Yaz, I'm sorry.'

'What for?'

Caitlin didn't reply.

She exited the car park and disappeared through the hotel gates. Helen rolled Caitlin's mysterious non-message to Yaz around in her head. What had she meant? Sorry for spoiling the weekend that Yaz had organised or something more? Shivering in spite of the full glare of the afternoon sun, Helen turned to face the hotel but she had taken no more than a few steps when she spotted Aiden.

'I've been looking for you everywhere.'

'I've only just got back.'

'I saw. A showdown with Caitlin?' Helen nodded. 'Are you okay? She hasn't told her brother about us has she?'

'She says not.'

'And you believe her?'

Helen nodded. 'I'm too terrified not to.'

'You don't look terrified.'

'I prefer to keep my worrying on the inside.' Helen wanted a hug and to be told everything was going to be all right, and yet the thought that it might come from Aiden unnerved her.

'I thought you'd be gone by now,' she said blinking away the tiredness in her eyes.

'We're all packed and ready,' replied Aiden. 'I just talked the lads into giving me an extra half an hour to look for you. It's cost me a two-hundred-quid bottle of cognac but it was worth it just to see your face again.' He gently grazed his hand against Helen's cheek. She recoiled.

'I told you this morning. I can't do this.'

'Can't do what exactly? I didn't dream last night, did I? We did kiss.'

'And I regret it.'

'That's the guilt talking, not you.'

'This is so easy for you, isn't it? You really think that a week before my wedding I'm going to leave the man I've lived with for nine years and jump straight into your arms.'

'No,' snapped Aiden, 'I think you'd rather just sit around making yourself feel bad for no reason first.'

'I thought you were being patient and understanding.'

'I was,' replied Aiden. 'I am. It's just that for the first time in a long while I know exactly what I want and it's frustrating that I can't have it.'

'You sound like a petulant schoolboy. Am I just another "thing" that you've got it into your head to desire?'

'It's not like that and you know it. I want you, Helen, I want you in my life right now. I know it's my fault that we split up. I know if I'd have done the right thing back when it really mattered we wouldn't be standing here having this ridiculous conversation. That's part of the reason I'm so keen. I'm just desperate to make things right.'

Helen's head was ready to explode. 'This is all too much!'

'I know,' said Aiden. 'And this is me trying to be restrained. Only you can make me like this, no one else.'

'Not even your ex-wife?'

'Not even my ex-wife.' He reached out for her hand. 'I'm trying to show you how committed I am to making a go of things. I know this is my last chance to prove I'm serious. This isn't just me playing at being romantic. This is me laying everything on the line. If you want me to give up my show I'll hand in my notice live on air tomorrow morning. If you want me to move out of London I'll be on the first train to Nottingham. Whatever it is you want you've got it.'

'How about time?'

A look of exasperation flashed across Aiden's face. 'You really know how to kill a grand gesture.'

'It's what I need though.'

'The resignation didn't float your boat?'

Helen shook her head.

'Fine, if time's what you want then it's yours. But know this: I'll be thinking about you every moment of every day until you call me.' He stepped forward ready to kiss her but Helen pulled away. 'I can't.'

'Maybe not,' murmured Aiden, 'but one day soon you will.'

17.

The girls were having tea at a table around the corner from the terrace. They were all wearing sunglasses and laughing at something Ros was saying. The moment they spotted Helen however the laughter stopped.

'I wish you wouldn't stop enjoying yourselves the second you see me. A girl could get paranoid.'

'How did it go?' asked Yaz. 'Did she pull a knife on you?'

'She was fine,' sighed Helen. 'We went to a pub down the road. Had a drink and a chat. The whole thing was actually quite civilised, she even asked me to pass on her apologies to you. It's certainly a weight off my mind.'

'So you two have made up?'

'I wouldn't go that far. It would be more accurate to say that if I was still marrying Phil, Caitlin and I would have chosen to turn over a new leaf. But as we're not, the point is sort of academic, although I am relieved to have the number of people in the world who hate my guts down to zero.'

'But the Phil situation remains the same?'

Helen nodded. 'She said she hadn't called him but

183

who knows? I'm not even sure it makes a difference now the wedding's off.'

The girls fell into an uneasy silence, looking to Yaz for guidance.

'We were thinking that we'd go in to lunch now if you're hungry.'

'I'm ravenous.'

'Good,' said Yaz. 'Then let's do it.'

Sick of being the sole topic of conversation Helen made sure to focus on what the girls had been up to as they made their way over to the restaurant. While they regaled her with tales of plunge pools, high-pitched screaming and stern reprimands from spa attendants, she succeeded in tucking her problems out of sight and enjoying the weekend for what it was meant to be.

They were disappointed to discover that all the tables on the terrace were taken but just then a group sitting outside left and with the best part of a dozen women simultaneously pleading to be given the table once it was cleared the waiter didn't stand a chance of refusing.

Seated in the sunshine, with a huge plate of prawn and avocado salad in front of her and a final bottle of champagne on its way to the table Helen felt her spirits lift but as she opened her mouth to take her first forkful of food she heard her phone vibrate as it received a text message.

She tried to ignore it, reasoning that there was no spam text worth delaying food as good as that on her plate for, but after a moment she automatically reached for her phone.

She looked at the screen. She didn't recognise the number and yet for reasons she couldn't begin to pinpoint she was convinced that she knew who the text was from.

'Are you okay?' asked Yaz topping up Helen's water glass.

Helen waved the glass away. 'I'm fine. It's just . . . it's just . . . it's just that this text . . . well, I think it's from Phil.'

Yaz was confused. 'How do you mean?'

'It's from a number that's not in my phone but I'm absolutely sure it's from Phil.'

Yaz held out her hand. 'Let me take a look.'

Helen handed her phone to Yaz. 'Don't open it.'

'Why not?'

'Because who knows what it says? What if the text is asking if I'm free to talk? I'm the world's worst liar. If I talk to him he'll know right away something's up.'

'But why do you think he needs to talk to you?' asked Lorna. 'If he's anything like my Dez, chances are he's texting to remind you to record the Grand Prix for him. Why don't you just read it and find out?'

Helen shook her head. 'I've just got a bad feeling about it.'

'What?' said Lorna, 'You don't think they've had some kind of accident do you?'

'No, if it was something like that he'd phone and there are no missed calls. I can't explain but the more I think about it the more I don't want to read this text. I'm going to leave it until I've seen him tonight and told him everything.'

'You don't think he already knows, do you?' said Yaz anxiously. 'Caitlin could have been lying about not contacting him.'

'She'd have nothing to gain.'

'In that case,' said Yaz. 'Give me the phone and if it's something you need to know I'll tell you.'

'And have to spend the rest of the day trying not to read meaning into your every action? No thanks.' Helen gave in. 'Okay, I'll read it and deal with the consequences.'

With the whole table watching her intently Helen manoeuvred her thumb into position but it refused to press the button that would reveal the contents of the text.

'I just can't do it,' she said.

Before Helen could voice her opposition Yaz snatched up the phone, opened the text and smiled.

'What?'

'You don't want to know,' teased Yaz.

'Of course I do.'

'It's not bad news.'

'So what does it say?'

Yaz handed the phone back to Helen and as her eyes locked on the screen she wanted to smile and cry at the same time.

Ros leaned in to take a peek. 'What does it say?'

Helen wiped her eyes. 'It says: "I love you Spoonface." ' With bated breath her friends waited for an explanation. 'It's the pet name Phil gave me years ago.'

Yaz laughed. 'We gathered that. Why Spoonface?'

Helen shrugged. 'He made it up and it stuck. He only ever calls me it when I'm sad or moody or worried. It's his way of relieving the tension.'

'And what's your pet name for him?'

'I've never felt like he's needed anything other than Phil,' said Helen quietly

'Why does everything have to be so difficult?' she said eventually. 'Why can't things be straightforward?' How desperately she had wanted to receive some form of communication from Phil and now that she had, it just made things worse.

'What should I do? Reply or leave it?'

Yaz spoke first. 'Leave it. He won't think anything of it.'

'But I always reply. What if he calls?'

'Just ignore it. There could be a million and one reasons why you didn't take the call.'

Helen wasn't convinced. 'I should call him.'

'And say what?'

'I don't know.'

'But you said yourself that you're the world's worst liar.'

'Then I'd better improve,' said Helen snatching up the phone once again, 'because right now I've not got much choice.'

Clutching her phone, Helen headed across the terrace towards one of the benches overlooking the river.

The afternoon sun was fierce and Helen felt her

brow dampen with perspiration. A middle-aged couple stood watching their two young children skimming stones across the surface of the water. Helen envied them. She wished she could be enjoying the pleasant surroundings and the beautiful weather without a care in the world instead of having to make a telephone call which could completely wreck everything she held dear.

She called up Phil's number and was ready to press down on the call button when the phone rang. She checked the screen.

'Hi, Mum, everything okay?'

'I'm fine, sweetie. I've just finished washing up and thought I'd call you before I go and have a sit in the garden. Are you having a nice weekend?'

'Yes, it's great. The weather's beautiful.'

'And how have those treatment things been?'

'Wonderful. Really relaxing.'

'Are you okay? You don't sound like your usual self.'

'I'm fine,' said Helen quickly. 'Just a bit tired. We had a late night and I still haven't recovered.'

'You shouldn't be having late nights this close to the wedding. Not if you want to look your best for next Saturday. The week before I married your father I was in bed for nine o'clock every night.'

'And every day you were up at six for your morning constitutional.'

'Left out of Granny's house, all the way along Spencer Street, right again at Larch Crescent, all the way along Radcliffe Street and back home in time to make